HELD

HELD

EDEET RAVEL

annick press
toronto + new york + vancouver

Edited by Barbara Berson
Cover and interior elements designed by Sheryl Shapiro

Annick Press Ltd.

We acknowledge the support of the Canada Council for the Arts, the Ontario Arts Council, and the Government of Canada through the Canada Book Fund (CBF) for our publishing activities.

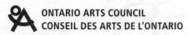

ONTARIO ARTS COUNCIL
CONSEIL DES ARTS DE L'ONTARIO

Cataloging in Publication

Ravel, Edeet, 1955-
        Held / by Edeet Ravel.

ISBN 978-1-55451-283-6 (bound).—ISBN 978-1-55451-282-9 (pbk.)

        I. Title.

PS8585.A8715H45 2011   jC813'.54   C2010-907055-0

Distributed in Canada by:
Firefly Books Ltd.
66 Leek Crescent
Richmond Hill, ON
L4B 1H1

Published in the U.S.A. by Annick Press (U.S.) Ltd.
Distributed in the U.S.A. by:
Firefly Books (U.S.) Inc.
P.O. Box 1338
Ellicott Station
Buffalo, NY 14205

Printed in Canada

Visit us at: www.annickpress.com
Visit Edeet Ravel at: www.edeet.com

for John

Washington, D.C.
Monday, 4:00 a.m.

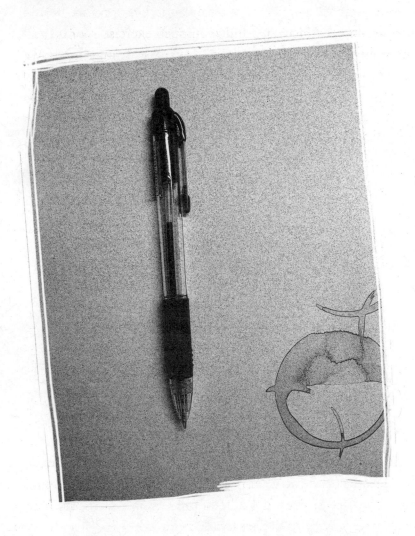

You've asked me to tell you everything. You've brought me to the best hotel in Washington, D. C., you've given me the hotel's best suite. There are flowers in every room, gift baskets on every table. There's a fireplace in the living room, heated tiles around the Jacuzzi, a fully equipped exercise room. I can order any meal I want, any time I want it. I imagine movie stars staying in these rooms, or famous world leaders.

I'm not alone. There's an armed guard outside my suite, a bodyguard on the terrace. Twice a day a nurse arrives to take my blood pressure, and every afternoon a psychologist named Monica comes to visit. My mom joins me for meals and usually spends the night in the guest bedroom, though she has her own suite one floor down.

You've told me the guards are there to protect me and that I'm free to do as I please. I'm not a prisoner. I can see anyone, go anywhere. I need only pick up the phone and make my desires known. But you suggested, courteously, that I remain indoors for a few days—it's safer for me, you said, and of course I understand that it's simpler for you. You reminded me that people from the media have infiltrated the hotel and are waiting for an opportunity to pounce on me, and that the crowds outside are barely manageable.

The laptop you've given me sits on the polished dining room table. My instructions are to write a detailed account of my experiences. When I'm finished, you'll let me go home.

I notice that you've emptied the bar. I assume you would have emptied it even if I'd been old enough to drink. You don't want anything to distract me from my task.

Looking down from the terrace, I can see the crowds on the street holding signs and banners and enormous posters with my face printed on them. "*I love you, Chloe,*" the signs say. The bodyguard tells me that entire families have come to Washington to welcome me home; they've flocked in from every part of the country.

How can they love me? They don't know me.

I can also see the media people, wandering aimlessly between the camera stands, bored and impatient. They want me, but I'm not giving myself to them. Not yet.

Mom hopes that in a few days we'll be able to fly home. She's been giving interviews and press conferences, and she tells me about the people she's met, the requests we've had from TV celebrities, publishers, and magazines, the wild sums of money I'm being offered for my story. She describes the small army of journalists who follow her everywhere, bombarding her with urgent questions.

We don't discuss what happened to me. Not because she's afraid to ask, but because she knows I'm not ready to talk about it. Or maybe what I'm not ready for is sorting out what I do and don't want her to know.

Thousands of gifts keep pouring in. The gifts are delivered to Mom's suite: clothes, luxury getaways, every sort of pretty object. She's keeping as many as she can manage for me and my friends; the rest are being redirected to charity. On my first day here she brought me a whole pile of outfits from the best boutiques, but I haven't tried any of them on yet. I'm still wearing the track pants and T-shirt they gave me at the clinic. Room service takes them away at bedtime, and when I wake up they're on the marble table in the outer foyer, cleaned and neatly folded.

But this isn't a vacation. You've brought me to this hotel for a reason: you need information. You told me to write down everything that happened to me from the day I was taken hostage to the day of my release. I have to record every detail of the past four months, no matter how small. You showed me magazines with cover stories about me; you told me the entire country was devastated by my ordeal.

After lunch the psychologist drops in. We talk about the weather, about what I'll do when I get home, about getting back to school and catching up on what I've missed. I've spoken to Angie once, and to my grandparents. I haven't gone on Facebook, I haven't contacted anyone else. I told everyone I was tired.

But the real reason is that I'm not entirely ready to return to my old life.

I'm sitting on the king-sized bed now, writing on the hotel's gold-and-blue stationery. What I'm writing will not be seen by you, will not be read by you. Even if you've installed a camera in these rooms, you won't be able to see my small, abbreviated handwriting, which I'm shielding with my body.

On the laptop you gave me, I'll produce another report, the one you will see. It will be factual, concise, accurate. It will not be complete.

But here, on pale-blue, gold-engraved paper, I will write the real story. The one you'll never read.

CHAPTER 1

I was taken hostage in Greece on the third of August.

I was working at a summer volunteer program with my friend Angie, just outside Athens. *My friend Angie*—I look at those words, and they seem to belong to someone else. It's as if I were a ghost, drifting through a world I've left behind and can never reclaim.

A volunteer program abroad was my idea, but Angie and I decided on Greece together, mostly because the photos on the websites we checked out were so beautiful—white domes, gold sand, every shade of blue. Angie, who loves to paint, said the colors would inspire her, and I remembered the Greek myths my father used to read to me; I still had the books, and I'd browsed through them often over the years. Athena, Apollo, Aphrodite. Labyrinths, adventures, transformations.

Mom was also enthusiastic about Greece; she's a dance teacher and choreographer, and in her twenties she traveled to Europe and the Far East to learn about indigenous dances. Greece was her favorite stop, and it was one of the reasons she'd named me Chloe—after a ballet, *Daphnis and Chloe*, based on a Greek story.

We landed in Athens at the beginning of June. The volunteer supervisor picked us up at the airport and drove us to one of the city's suburbs, where we'd be teaching kids at a community center. The *katikies*, as our rooms were called, were pretty dismal, and we soon found out that we'd also be expected to wash dishes, mop floors, and take out garbage.

But the cute kids and the amazing surroundings more than made up for any disappointments. I taught dance and gymnastics to a class of well-behaved, enthusiastic girls, and Angie worked in the arts and crafts room. On our free days we joined excursions organized by the center. We explored islands, wandered down narrow streets with vine-covered houses, went scuba-diving, and stuffed ourselves with Mediterranean food. We watched the sun set in Oia; we watched the sun rise behind the Parthenon.

Our favorite fellow volunteers were Camille and Peter, tall blond twins from Norway who loved to joke and laugh. We bonded on the first day, when Camille's suitcase was accidentally shipped to Japan and we told her to help herself to whatever we had. Angie developed an instant, hopeless crush on Peter, who unfortunately for her already had a girl-friend back home.

A crush was nothing new for Angie, who's always falling madly and usually hopelessly in love. Not that guys don't like her—on the contrary, she has a great personality and she's gorgeous; her Argentinean mother used to be a model and Angie inherited her charisma.

But she tends to fall for unattainable types—ski instructors who are engaged, university students who consider her a kid (her father teaches at Northwestern and every semester he has a party for his grad students), or some guy she's seen in a dance competition on TV and decided she has to meet, even if he lives on some distant ranch in Canada.

Angie's disappointment that Peter had a girlfriend was

alleviated by the constant attention that came our way from the local male population, who had never heard of the word *shy*, in Greek or in English. Angie enjoyed flirting back, which only made them bolder.

In my book, they were stalkers, but Angie said I needed to be more open-minded to "mating customs in other cultures," a phrase that made all four of us—especially Camille—laugh hysterically. "Your friend does not like us," the guys would say to Angie in my presence. "Why is it?"

But it wasn't true that I didn't like them. They were simply too random for me; I couldn't trust some stranger, no matter how good-looking, who appeared out of nowhere. Camille said I wasn't at ease with guys because I'd grown up without a father or brother, but Angie insisted that my problem was an obsession with control and order. I had to be in charge, she said. I had to plan and organize everything, including who I met.

Classes ended on the first of August. We were sorry to be leaving the community center, and so were the children. They gave us little presents and asked us to stay in Greece forever.

Our return flight was three days away. We were allowed to stay in our *katikies* and explore on our own, as long as we were back before dark. We asked Camille and Peter to join us, but they were meeting friends in Italy. We hugged one another good-bye and they made us promise to visit them in Norway.

On our first free day Angie suggested we head out without a plan and let things unfold. We'd get on a bus, see where it took us, have an adventure.

I resisted. "We have to at least know where we're going," I said.

It's always been like that: we're almost identical in every other way, but when it comes to being organized we're opposites. Angie's room is like a big jumble sale, and every few days she'd call and beg me to come over and help her find something crucial that she'd lost. I'd be like one of those professionals who tidy houses—I'd spend two hours folding her clothes, putting papers into neat piles, arranging all her paints and pastels. A week later, the room would be back to its usual post-tornado state.

It was the same with going out places. Angie was laid-back, but I liked to know where we were headed, how long everything would take, and what we had to bring with us.

Especially now that we were in a foreign country and didn't even speak the language.

But Angie was very persuasive. She said she'd had enough of schedules and rushing around. She wanted to relax. Reluctantly, I agreed to get on a bus and see what happened.

The day was jinxed. We got lost in a sketchy town in the middle of nowhere, Angie's sandal strap broke, a scary old man began to follow us, we were hot, we couldn't find water, and we had a terrible meal at a dumpy restaurant that left us feeling sick.

To top it off, Angie had an asthma attack and I got my period.

And when we returned to our *katikies* we found that all our things had been moved to another room so the place could be cleaned, and several items were missing. We began to fight.

I started it. "This is all your fault," I said angrily. "We could have had a great time if you'd let me plan the day. Why do you think they invented guidebooks?"

Angie's cheeks, usually pale as porcelain, turned bright red. Poor Angie, her face has always revealed exactly what she's feeling. She used to joke about it, calling herself the living emoticon.

"Just because I'm not a control freak like you," she struck back. "I like to take risks, okay? I don't want to live my life like an automaton. At least I'll have a life."

I should have apologized, but I was too stubborn and grouchy. "Well, I want to see the Nemesis Temple tomorrow," I announced. "It means waking up on time and following a schedule. If you'd rather sleep in, I can go on my own."

"Fine, go on your own," Angie snapped. She slid into the narrow bed and turned her back on me.

In ten years of being friends, we could have counted our fights on one hand. Neither of us liked conflict, and we agreed on almost everything. We liked the same music, the same movies, the same people. Angie has an older brother and sister, but they were already in high school when she was born, and they'd both moved out by the time she was in first grade. And I'm an only child; my father died when I was six and Mom never remarried. Angie became my surrogate sister and I became hers.

But we were tired and disappointed that night, and we let

it out by sniping at each other. I blame myself. I started the fight, and I kept it going. I could have said I was sorry or joked about my obsessive personality, but I didn't.

If we hadn't fought, I'd still be the same person I was then. None of this would have happened. Because of our fight, my life was going to change forever.

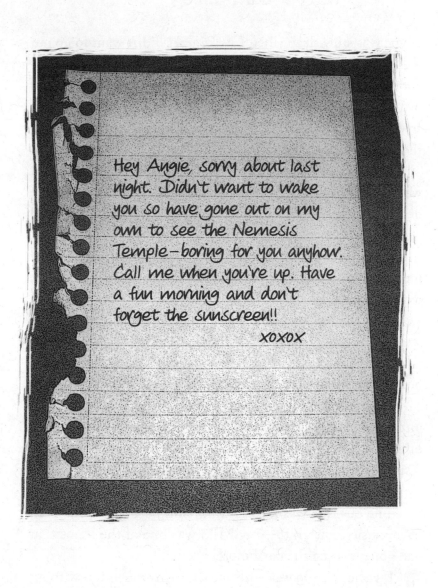

CHAPTER 2

Angie was still asleep when I woke up. I didn't want to go out while we were still fighting, but I knew she might sleep for another two or three hours, and the *katikies* weren't the kind of place you wanted to hang around in. The small rooms smelled of wax beans, and flies buzzed around garbage pails at the end of the hallway.

I could have waited at the café around the corner, but it would be boring on my own, and besides, I wasn't ready to deal with the over-friendliness of the Mediterranean male without backup.

I decided to set out for the temple myself and then hopefully meet Angie at a beach near Marathon, which my guidebook recommended.

I got dressed, packed my knapsack, left Angie a note, and stepped outside. I was full of energy, the kind you feel when you crave a new experience, a new setting. Luckily, there was a bus to Marathon every half hour.

At first it felt strange, even a little scary, being completely on my own in a foreign country. But there were plenty of other tourists at the station, and I smiled at the kids of an Asian couple who were standing next to me in line. They smiled back and asked me where I was from.

The bus ride was long and hot and boring. I didn't even have music to listen to—my MP3 was one of the items that had gone missing the day before.

I wished Angie was with me. It wasn't much fun without

her—there was no one to talk to, no one to laugh with, no one jumping up and exclaiming when a vast herd of goats suddenly appeared against the horizon.

The bus finally came to a stop and we clambered out. The Nemesis Temple was off the beaten track, according to my guidebook—that was one of the reasons I wanted to go there: it wouldn't be packed with tourists. When we'd visited the Temple of Poseidon the previous week we felt we were at a football stadium.

The only way to get to the site, which was nine miles from the station, was either to hitch a ride with another tourist or take a taxi. No one else seemed to be going to the temple, and a toothless taxi driver who looked about a hundred years old called out to me, "Where you want? I go, I go."

I accepted the offer and fifteen minutes later I was at the temple. The driver was ready to wait for me, but I didn't want to feel rushed. There were a few other tourists there, and I was sure one of them would be able to give me a lift back.

The site was breathtaking. I wished I'd waited for Angie; she would have loved it. The temple stones were surrounded by dense layers of olive-green trees that seemed golden in the sunlight, and beyond the temple lay the ruins of the town of Rhamnous, a maze of low stone walls. In the distance, the sapphire sea and a ribbon of misty mountains merged with a cloudless sky.

I gazed at the ancient blocks of stone in the midst of the still landscape and tried to imagine what the temple had looked like two thousand years ago. The remains were as mysterious now as the temple itself must have been to its first worshippers. Nemesis—goddess of divine justice and vengeance.

I decided to look up bus schedules for Angie and text her; maybe she could meet me here instead of at the beach. I'd explore the city ruins in the meantime, or else wait for her at Marathon.

I was also hungry; luckily I'd brought some bread and cheese with me. I wandered down the road, looking for somewhere to sit down. I found a boulder near some bushes, settled myself on it, and began entering bus times on my phone.

I was facing away from the road and didn't hear a car stop beside me, or if I did, I didn't pay any attention to it. I was absorbed in texting Angie.

All at once an arm grabbed my waist and the phone fell from my hands. It was so sudden that I cried out before I knew what I was feeling. Instinctively I resisted. Someone was trying to pull me, and I tried to pull back. I didn't succeed. I was dragged into a car and the car began to move.

It took me a few seconds to sort out my basic physical situation: I was sitting on a car seat and I'd been blindfolded, though not very efficiently. Someone had removed my watch and was holding my wrists behind me.

I was sure there had been a mistake. I've heard that denial is the first response to any frightening situation. I told myself that this was a practical joke, or a game, or something harmless and meaningless.

I said, "Hey, what's going on!"

A man's voice said, "If you cooperate, you won't come to

any harm." He spoke casually, as if he were discussing the weather. I continued thinking, *This is a mistake, I'll be released any minute.*

Then I thought, *Someone must have seen what happened— one of the tourists will call the police. In the meantime, just do everything they say and you'll be fine.* I was still in denial, though I was aware that my heart was beating very fast.

Then the man said, "Take off your jeans. Leave your underwear on." He seemed to have a British accent along with his foreign one.

It's a mugging, I thought. *Just some poor locals who want my jeans and my watch and my money.*

At the same time, the car seemed to be very spacious— I couldn't feel the seat in front of me. The smell of the car and its size made me think it was a limo. Well, maybe it was a stolen limo, and the thieves had decided to add mugging to their crime spree.

The man let go of my wrists and I began to fumble with my jeans. My fingers felt clumsy and I was afraid that I wasn't removing them fast enough. It was at that moment—when I realized that I had to do exactly as I was told—that my denial turned to terror. I understood very suddenly that I was in trouble, and I began to tremble.

All the same, I clung to the thought that they were mugging me. Maybe now that they had my jeans and watch and knapsack, they'd let me go. They'd throw me out of the car, and I'd be safe. They had told me to keep my underwear on. That was a good sign.

"Put on this skirt," the man said in the same casual voice.

I felt something landing on my knees, and I instinctively recoiled with fear of the unknown. Through the bottom of the blindfold I saw a heap of black fabric. I was relieved that it really was a skirt and not a snake or a rat. I found the elastic waist, and pulled it on. It was ankle-length.

Why a skirt? I wondered. Why didn't they just throw me out of the car, once they had my jeans?

A sickening answer came to me: they were taking me to be a sex slave somewhere, and they were disguising me, or dressing me up. Maybe they were taking me to some Middle Eastern country, where women had to wear long dresses.

Then I remembered that terrorists sometimes dressed their victims in certain colors before executing them. I let out a cry, and my trembling intensified. Years of dance and gymnastics made me think of myself as having good control over my body, but I was shaking so violently that my leg knocked against the leg of the man sitting next to me.

I felt something being pulled over my head, and I thought at first that it was a sack of some sort and that I was going to be shot on the spot. But a second later it fell past my head, onto my shoulders. It seemed to be a kind of poncho. My running shoes and socks were pulled off and I realized I was whimpering, in spite of myself. My shoes were replaced by sandals.

Now that he'd finished dressing me, the man tied my hands behind my back. My whimpers turned to sobbing. I wasn't being mugged, I was being given a new identity. And that meant that they had plans for me. "Please, please," I begged between sobs.

The man said, "Don't panic. Just do as we say and you won't be harmed."

"Please let me go," I pleaded. I knew no one was ever released by criminals because they asked to be let go, but it was almost an instinct, to plead.

I tried to force myself to calm down. I needed to focus on a plan of escape, I needed to be alert and calm so that I could free myself. The blindfold was loosely tied; if I rubbed the side of my head against my shoulder, it would slip off altogether. I'd have to find a way to make a run for it. I reminded myself that I was a fast runner.

On the other hand, it would be hard running in sandals, especially loose ones like these. Maybe that was the reason they'd taken away my running shoes.

But no matter where we stopped, there were bound to be people not too far away. Greece was not the Nevada Desert, after all. If I ran, someone would see me, someone would help me.

I tried not to think about what might happen to me if I didn't get away. The important thing was to find a way to escape. I told myself that if they were planning to drug me or shoot me, they would have done it by now.

"Where are you taking me?" I asked.

"You've been taken hostage for a prisoner release," the man said.

It was as if he was talking about someone else—partly

because his voice was so calm and partly because I couldn't make sense of the words.

Prisoner release—he must mean a prisoner in the U.S. They were terrorists, and they wanted one of their friends to be freed.

I began to cry. "I can give you money," I said. Not that Mom and I had any money to spare, but Angie's parents would help out, and our beautiful old house could be mortgaged ...

But it was hopeless: this wasn't a kidnapping for ransom. That's not what they were after, and my offer was met by silence.

I wondered how many people were in the car, apart from the man and the driver. There was no way of telling.

"Is this a limo?" I asked, not expecting a reply.

"Yes," the man said.

I thought of organized crime, international power. Who knew if they were telling me the truth about the prisoner exchange? It might only be a way of hiding their real purpose. Maybe they were planning to sell me as a sex slave to some lunatic billionaire, and this was his car. Maybe he was driving. I had to escape somehow.

"Do you have any medical conditions?" the man asked. In spite of his accent, his English seemed to be good. But the formal language, and the question itself, gave my imagination more horrors to feed on, and I thought—*Oh God, they want to experiment on me, or kill me for my organs.*

This was my chance, and I had to think fast. But I couldn't think fast enough. "I'm diabetic," I blurted out stupidly.

As soon as I said it, I knew they'd see through that lie, and they did.

"I don't see any insulin in your bag," the man said, sounding almost amused. "No one wants to hurt you or do anything to you," he added, reading my mind. "Try to relax. I want to give you some Valium, and I need to know if you're on anything else."

At least his voice wasn't aggressive. But was it really Valium he wanted to give me, or something more deadly? Heroin, maybe—so he could turn me into an addict ...

"Don't imagine the worst," he said, reading my mind again. "So I take it you're in good health—aside from the diabetes?" He was teasing me, and that might have reassured me a little, but I was too terrified.

At least they didn't want me to die. Not yet, anyhow.

I nodded miserably. For the first time I understood the word *terrorist*. Before I knew what was happening, I felt a needle in my arm. I began to scream, then my screams faded into a blurry daze. The drug was working; I felt sleepy and confused. I leaned my head back on the seat and shut my eyes.

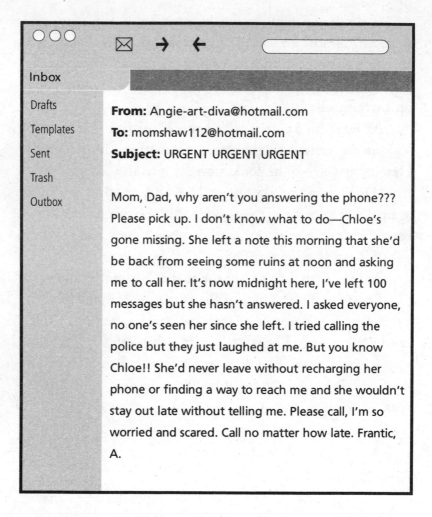

From: Angie-art-diva@hotmail.com
To: momshaw112@hotmail.com
Subject: URGENT URGENT URGENT

Mom, Dad, why aren't you answering the phone???
Please pick up. I don't know what to do—Chloe's
gone missing. She left a note this morning that she'd
be back from seeing some ruins at noon and asking
me to call her. It's now midnight here, I've left 100
messages but she hasn't answered. I asked everyone,
no one's seen her since she left. I tried calling the
police but they just laughed at me. But you know
Chloe!! She'd never leave without recharging her
phone or finding a way to reach me and she wouldn't
stay out late without telling me. Please call, I'm so
worried and scared. Call no matter how late. Frantic,
A.

CHAPTER 3

I don't know how long the drive was. It could have been half an hour or it could have been several hours. I was thirsty, my shoulders ached, my legs had fallen asleep. But my heart was no longer pounding like mad and I wasn't trembling. The drug made me groggy and unfocused. Horrifying images of being beheaded or buried alive drifted away like clouds.

"We're here," the man said. He spoke as if nothing extraordinary was taking place. "We'll be taking a plane. But first you'll need a wig and a hat."

The man untied my hands and placed a long-haired wig on my head. I could see black strands from the edges of my blindfold. How did they know I'd be blond? Or had they brought a variety of wigs with them, I wondered sleepily. Red, blue, purple …

This is your last chance to escape, a voice in my head reminded me. My hands were free now; that would help me run. But I could barely move my legs, never mind trying to make a dash for it.

I felt a large, floppy hat slide down my forehead and sunglasses slipped on over my blindfold. I thought I heard a woman's voice muttering in another language, but I was no longer sure whether I was awake or dreaming.

The man and the woman—or so I imagined—led me to a set of stairs. I now understood why they'd tied the blindfold so loosely: it was so I could see where I was going. I climbed the four or five stairs to the plane with the help of my captors, who held me by my elbows as if I was sick and they were looking after me.

There are bound to be other passengers, I thought. I was very mixed up. They'd given me something stronger than Valium, I realized. Nothing made any sense.

The man said, "Mind your head, the ceiling's low." In spite of my drugged state, this was the most terrifying moment yet. The plane's low ceiling—it was under five feet—made me think of a coffin.

"Do you need a lavatory?" he asked. The word confused me, and it took me a second to realize that he was asking me if I needed to use the toilet. "It's your last chance in a while," he added, misinterpreting my hesitation.

I nodded. I was led, crouching, to a toilet and handed a small box of tissues. "No one's watching you," the man said, but I didn't hear a door shut, and of course I had no way of knowing if he was telling me the truth. He wasn't being considerate, I thought, only practical—some people can't pee if they're being watched. It made no difference to me; I was too drugged to care about anything other than keeping my balance.

I had to gather the long skirt up, and I thought for a minute that I was going to fall over, but the woman caught me—so much for not watching. I knew it was her because her hair brushed my cheek as she steadied me. I also thought I detected a faint odor of perfume or scented shampoo.

Somehow I managed to get through what seemed like a very complicated process. I even remembered to remove my tampon—luckily I never had heavy periods, and there was a just-in-case pad in place. *Just in case of kidnapping*, I thought vaguely.

I was glad after that to sink into a large, comfortable passenger seat. The claustrophobia dissolved, and I had the drugged sensation that everything would work out. Someone reclined it, and I drifted off into a deep sleep.

When I woke up I thought at first that I was in the *katikies* with Angie and that everything was dark because it was the middle of the night. Then I realized that I was sitting up in a vehicle of some sort. The memory of what had happened came flooding back to me. It was dark because I was blindfolded.

For a moment it seemed that my entire body was tied to the seat, and I let out a short, involuntary scream. Then I realized it was only a seatbelt that was strapped diagonally across me, and in fact my arms were free, though I felt very weak. I could tell from the sounds and the motion of the vehicle that I was no longer on the plane. Had there really been a plane?

It was intensely hot in the vehicle, and I couldn't remember ever being so thirsty. "I need water," I said. My voice came out in a raspy whisper.

I was handed a bottle of water and I gulped it down without caring whether it was drugged or poisoned. If I didn't have water I'd die anyhow.

Try to escape, I reminded myself. But I knew it was hopeless; I couldn't even hold on to the empty water bottle and it slid to the floor. At least the hat and wig were gone. I wondered what that meant.

"Where am I?" I asked.

"In a van. We're almost there." It was the same man; he was clearly the one in charge of this part of the abduction. I noticed again that he had a British accent, along with his other accent—Greek, or maybe something else.

The heat in the van was making me sweat and the blindfold began to slide down my nose. "My blindfold is loose," I said. I was afraid it would fall off by mistake, and I'd see my hostage-taker. I knew from hundreds of movies and TV shows that if you saw criminals, they had to kill you.

He reached over and tightened the blindfold. As his hands touched my hair, I had one of those flash memories—a mother at a birthday party tying a blindfold on my eyes for Pin the Tail on the Donkey. For a split second I could smell the birthday cake, and I even remembered the dress I was wearing: dark-pink satin with black buttons.

If only this were a game too, and any minute now someone would pull my blindfold off and laugh at the joke they'd played on me.

I felt more helpless and vulnerable than I would have believed possible. I didn't even know what country I was in—what if we were in Iraq? Or some other distant, war-torn place?

I began to cry uncontrollably. I was sure it was over for me. No government ever released prisoners under pressure from hostage-takers—it would only encourage more hostage-taking. My hostage-takers would fail, and they'd kill me. That is, if their intention really was to free a prisoner. Maybe it was something even worse. I thought of Mom, and what it would be like for her to lose me. I was unbearably sad for her, and for my grandparents, and of course for myself.

The man handed me a tissue and said, "We're not in a war zone. You'll be safe." How did he do that—how did he read my mind? My face must have betrayed me, just like Angie's. Or else he was experienced and knew exactly what hostages went through, step by step, detail by detail. Because he'd done it before. And I was only the next victim.

A hundred thousand women disappear each year—Mom had said that in the airport. She was warning us to be careful, not to trust strangers, not to take chances. We'd both laughed. And even Mom had smiled at her overprotective, overly anxious warning.

And now it had happened to me. I had disappeared. I wondered when Angie would realize that I'd vanished, when she'd call the police. I said I'd be home by noon, and she knew I'd never change my plans without telling her. Even if I lost my phone, I'd find a way to reach her. She must have tried calling me all day. She'd have contacted her parents by now, and I was sure they'd call the police. Not that it mattered. It was already too late.

Poor Angie! She'd blame herself. She was such a sensitive and emotional person—how would she cope? I thought of all the TV shows we'd watched together in which police detectives had to find serial killers before they tortured their next victim to death. Angie always covered her eyes when there was any sort of violence or suspense. Even if she knew there'd be a happy ending, she couldn't bear to watch.

At least I'd left her that note. It would be a million times worse if she thought I'd gone off on my own because I was angry with her. "I left Angie a note," I said out loud. I was glad the man wouldn't know what I was talking about. He couldn't really read my mind.

Did they have my phone, I wondered, or was it on the road where I'd dropped it? Maybe the phone was right there in the van. If I weren't so weak, I could try to overpower the man—I'd taken two years of karate when I quit gymnastics, and I was very strong. I wondered how long the effects of the drug would last. Maybe they planned to keep me permanently drugged.

Wherever we were, it must be close to the equator to be this hot. How far could small planes fly? Hundreds of miles, at least. Maybe thousands. I felt a horrible, hollow terror in the pit of my stomach, as if I'd been let loose in outer space. I began to cry again.

"Take deep breaths, you'll feel better," the man said. "Twenty more minutes. Just hang in there."

I didn't breathe in deeply—I wasn't going to let him control my breathing as well as everything else—but I tried to focus my mind, the way I used to do during gymnastics competitions. He was being kind to me, and I wanted to show him that I appreciated it, so he'd go on being kind.

"Where are you taking me?" I asked. My voice sounded hoarse and strange, and I wasn't sure the words had been clear.

"To a place we've prepared."

"Are you going to sell me?" I asked.

"No."

I knew he could be lying. I clutched the seat handles as if they were my last anchor to the ordinary world. I noticed that the poncho they'd given me smelled of mothballs. Why had they dressed me in this outfit? I had to push away terrifying answers. Maybe they belonged to a strange satanic cult, and this was part of the sacrificial costume. I began to tremble again.

Don't imagine the worst, the man had said. They had given me these clothes so no one would recognize me, that was all.

"I'm afraid," I said out loud. I felt a little better, saying those words, and I repeated them. "I'm afraid."

"Yes, I know."

"Are you some sort of cult?"

"No, that's just in the movies."

It was like a gift, when he said that. He was joking with me—he was stepping out of his role. He was telling me that we were two human beings, as well as captive and captor.

If he was lying, he wouldn't have made that comment, I thought.

"Is it because I'm from the United States?" I asked. "Are you ... militants?" I didn't use the word *terrorists* because I knew that terrorists thought of themselves as fighters for a just cause.

"You're not in any danger," he said, not answering my question.

If they were terrorists they'd have machine-guns, I told myself, but in fact I had no idea what sort of weapons they had, or how many of them there were, apart from the man, the driver, and the woman. Maybe the woman was the driver. Maybe there were only these two.

These two here, now, but he'd said "we." *To a place we've prepared.* He must have meant the group he belonged to.

It was hard to grasp. We were two strangers, but our lives were now inextricably tied to each other. My life was in his hands. I'd never been so closely connected to anyone, except maybe Mom, when I was little.

At least he hasn't tried anything, I thought. *He hasn't touched me.*

I remembered a movie I'd seen long ago on television. Natasha Richardson had played Patty Hearst, a heiress who'd been kidnapped by a crazy revolutionary group in the 1970s. She'd been locked in a tiny closet for months, and one of the men in the group had forced her to have sex with him.

I decided that if that happened I would shut myself off completely. I would pretend I was someone else, I would make it not matter. I was only sorry that I was a virgin, if that was going to be my first time.

No one had made a move so far, but no one had made a move on Patty Hearst either, at the start.

Could something have already happened on the plane, while I was drugged? No, I'd know.

Maybe he was gay. Or maybe he'd try something later … or was he keeping his hands off me because he was a religious Muslim?

Don't think, don't think, I told myself. And in fact everything was starting to feel unreal again. It was as if I was in some sort of waking dream or play, and none of it was really happening.

Yes, think, I instructed myself. I had to plan for whatever might happen. I couldn't fade away again.

I heard the sound of a lid turning and I smelled coffee. The man asked in the same placid voice, "Would you like coffee? Or a sandwich?" It was almost as if his voice was a mask—it didn't reveal what he was feeling or thinking.

I shook my head. Mom didn't drink coffee, and I'd never developed a taste for it. I wasn't hungry either. I still felt queasy from the drug—or maybe it was just stress.

"Well, here's a sandwich, in case you change your mind." The man placed what felt like a bread roll in my hand, and almost instinctively I bit into it. I was surprised to find that it was a brie sandwich. Not the sort of thing I would have expected, in the circumstances. The bread was also unusually fresh, and it tasted homemade.

Even though I was blindfolded, being held captive, and possibly in the hands of murderers, the delicious sandwich made me feel better. It's hard to believe how quickly you become accustomed to losing your freedom, being blindfolded, not knowing where you are or what's happening to you.

I wondered what time it was. Mom would know by now that I was missing. She'd be wild with worry—fearing the worst but trying to stay hopeful. *Mommy, mommy.* The word seemed to tear through my body. *Later*, I thought. *When I'm alone.*

"Does my mother know I'm alive?" I asked.

"Not yet," the man answered, and his inexpressive voice suddenly seemed cold and cruel.

The van came to a stop, and a second later I heard the door slide open.

I unbuckled myself and shifted in my seat. Every muscle in my body seemed to ache. It reminded me of my gymnastics days, but this was a different type of pain. I could barely stand up.

Once again the man and the woman took hold of my arms and led me out of the van. I heard the woman murmur, *Poor dear*, but her voice sounded like Mom's, and I decided I'd had an auditory hallucination. I hoped I wasn't losing my mind. "It's tension and fatigue—and chemicals," I said out loud. I hoped tension and fatigue and chemicals were also the reason I was talking to myself.

We entered a building that I imagined for some reason was an abandoned church. I heard someone emptying the contents of my knapsack on a table and rummaging through my things. Then a door slammed shut and it was quiet. They were gone. I hadn't even tried to escape.

U.S. Tourist Disappears in Greece

The discovery yesterday of a cell phone belonging to a U.S. teen-ager who disappeared on August 3 in Greece has heightened concern about the missing girl. Known for being responsible, 17-year-old Chloe Mills was last seen by fellow tourists at the Nemesis Temple in Rhamnous.

Chloe, a top high school student from Chicago, failed to return to her accommodations and was reported missing by classmate Angie Shaw. Both girls were spending the summer at a volunteer work program near Athens.

Police Sgt. Marco Papadopolous of the International Police Cooperation Division said that preliminary investigations are underway, but added that it is too early to call a search. He commented that young people often branch out on their own if they meet other like-minded tourists. However, the discovery of Chloe's phone on a side road is seen as a significant development.

A tearful Ms. Shaw said, "I know something's wrong. Chloe would never vanish without a word, not in a million years."

Reached at her Chicago home, Chloe's widowed mother, Allegra Mills, confirmed that the disappearance is out of character. "Chloe's always been responsible. She doesn't take risks," said a concerned Ms. Mills.

"I'm trying to be hopeful," she said. Ms. Mills is flying to Greece today to be closer to the investigation and to encourage the police to act quickly.

POST REPORT

CHAPTER 4

I took off my blindfold.

My surroundings were nothing like a church, of course. I was in what appeared to be a large, empty warehouse, about the size of a tennis court, with a cement floor, cement walls, and a very high ceiling. Small glass panes ran along the top of one of the walls.

There was a mattress on the floor, a bridge table, two folding chairs, a small fridge, a standing lamp, two shelves, a pail and mop, and a partition with saloon doors in the far corner. My things were scattered on the table, along with an empty notebook, a pen, three paperbacks, cutlery, a mug, a plate, and a sealed bottle of water.

My jeans were there too, draped over one of the chairs, and my running shoes had been set neatly on the floor, my socks tucked inside.

I opened the bottle of water and had a long drink. Then I pulled off the poncho and skirt and put on my jeans. I hated the long black skirt because it had made me think of satanic cults, and I rolled it up and stuffed it inside the pail.

I walked over to the saloon doors and pushed them open. Several cockroaches scurried into corners. I was facing a tiny cubicle with an oversized sink, very old and rusty, the kind you see in garages and cellars. Luckily, the toilet and shower stall next to the sink were in better shape. In fact, they both looked new.

The bathroom had been prepared for me. Several rolls of

toilet paper had been stacked on a shelf above the sink, along with a plastic cup, a toothbrush, a bar of soap, a small bottle of pale green liquid that I assumed was shampoo, and an unlabeled tube of toothpaste. A blue towel hung from a nail on the wall. I was grateful not to be locked in a closet, but there was something unspeakably depressing about these sad supplies.

I'd completely forgotten about my period, and no wonder— it had apparently stopped altogether.

I turned on the faucet and washed my hands and face. It seemed like a gift from heaven, just to be able to splash water on my face.

I went back to the table to see what they had taken. My passport, wallet, and camera were missing. My watch had also not been returned. A wave of nausea came over me, and I was afraid I was going to be sick. I sat down and lowered my head to my knees.

But lowering my head made me feel even worse. It was as if someone had turned on a switch in my brain and every horrific scene I'd seen on film or television flashed through my mind. Psychotic sadists who cut off the limbs of their victims one by one, skinned them alive … I realized that I was moaning.

The terror was unbearable, and I forced myself to repeat out loud what the man had told me: "Don't imagine the worst. Don't imagine the worst. You're not in any danger." I chanted the words over and over like a mantra, until the images began at last to recede.

I felt emotionally and physically drained. I was vaguely aware that I was hungry, but I was too tired to care. I glanced at the mattress. It was a large piece of hard foam, almost as wide as a double bed.

I had somehow failed to notice the typed note lying on a carefully folded army blanket at the edge of the mattress. I froze—there was something horribly spooky about seeing it now, as if it had appeared out of thin air. In my disorientation, I wondered whether someone was watching me through a hidden camera.

I crouched down, afraid to touch the small sheet of paper. The note said:

> *You are here for the purpose of a prisoner exchange. No harm will come to you. There is food in the refrigerator. I'll visit in a day or two to see that you have what you need. We regret the inconvenience.*

Regret the inconvenience! I almost laughed, but my laughter would have frightened me.

Under the folded army blanket there were two folded white sheets, a pillow, a pillowcase, and another blue towel. I made the bed, more or less, and lay down. I was a little chilly, and I covered myself with the blanket. I realized that the warehouse was air-conditioned.

I felt like the last person on the planet. No one knew where I was; no one had any way of finding me. I sat up and hugged my knees. I didn't want to sleep just yet.

My stomach began to rumble. I was starving. I walked over to the fridge and pulled at the heavy curved door. It was an old fridge, and the door stuck to the frame unless you pulled hard.

I expected to see a bottle of milk inside, a loaf of bread, maybe a container of yogurt. But the shelves were crammed with food.

I cleared the table and began taking out the different containers. There were four baked apples filled to the brim with raisins and almonds, rice pudding decorated with pistachio nuts arranged in a circle, a vegetable salad, a pasta salad, a fruit salad topped with curled chocolate, a bean mix sprinkled with dill, some sort of casserole, two dips, and a bowl of stuffed vine leaves, which I'd tasted on our first day in Greece and didn't like.

Odd, I thought, to give a prisoner such fine food. Creepy ... no, I wouldn't let myself get into a panic again. Still, it was the sort of thing you'd expect from a sex pervert—lock you up and then feed you delicacies. I shuddered, and a violent wave of homesickness swept over me. I wanted to be back in my bedroom, in my house, in my city. I wanted to be safe.

I stared at the gourmet dishes and wondered whether they were drugged. Maybe the note was intended to put me off guard. I'd eat the food, fall into a stupor, and then the pervert would come. He had probably paid them to kidnap me. I tried to shake off the idea that I'd been sold as a sex slave, but I couldn't get rid of it.

In the end my hunger, or fatigue, won out. I had to eat

eventually; if the food was drugged, there was nothing I could do about it. I dug into the rice pudding, eating it straight from the bowl. It was delicious, and I felt a little better.

I returned to the bed and pulled the blanket over me a second time. In a few seconds I was asleep.

Video of Tourist's Brutal Execution on YouTube

The video-sharing website YouTube has removed a lurid video showing the execution of 17-year-old Chloe Mills, a Chicago high school student who went missing in Greece on August 3.

U.S. officials are closely studying the video in order to determine its authenticity. The video was posted by a party calling itself "Al Qaeda Super Warriors." Several bloggers have reported viewing the video before it was removed, stating that it was "gruesome" and showed the young girl being repeatedly stabbed.

An honors student who excels in dance and gymnastics, Chloe vanished shortly after visiting a tourist site north of Athens. The discovery of her cell phone on a dirt road has added to fears she may have been abducted.

Chloe's mother, Allegra Mills, spoke to reporters from the airport in Athens. Ms. Mills, a dance teacher, arrived in Greece this morning with John Shaw, father of the missing teen's traveling companion, Angie Shaw, with the intention of urging authorities to step up the search for her daughter. "I know she's alive," said Ms. Mills, struggling to remain composed. "I'm sure of it. I would know if anything like that happened to her."

Ms. Shaw was unavailable for comment. Her father said, "She is distressed. We all are. We're waiting for news."

POST REPORT

CHAPTER 5

I can't be sure, but I think I slept for a long time. When I finally woke up I was very confused. I knew something significant had happened, but I didn't know what it was. When I remembered, I found it hard to believe that I hadn't dreamed it all. I was sure that any minute now the new reality would dissolve and I'd find myself in the *katikies* with Angie.

I jumped out of bed and flung myself at the warehouse door. I knew it would be locked, but I couldn't stop myself from trying to break it down.

It's hard to describe the loss of freedom, the feeling of being caged in. A huge, unbearable desire to get out comes over you, and the more aware you are that you can't go out, the more intense the desire becomes. I'd been locked in for only one night and it already felt endless. How would I survive if I was still here a week from now?

I looked despairingly at the windows, but they were too high to reach, even if I climbed on the table and chair, and they were probably too small for my body in any case. Besides, how would I lower myself on the other side?

I allowed myself now to think of Mom—I wanted to think of her. Imagining her response to my disappearance consoled me and broke my heart at the same time. She would do everything she could for me, but she'd be beside herself with worry and fear. Maybe by now she'd received word from my captors and knew at least that I was alive. If they were interested in a prisoner exchange, they'd have to announce that I was safe. And that would give her hope.

I sat on the bed with the notebook they'd given me and began listing happy memories. Our summers in Vermont, in a rented cottage by the lake. Shelburne Farms—was that where I'd seen the little red schoolhouse, or was it somewhere else?

Sunday dinners with my grandparents, followed by games around the fireplace.

Talent-show dances Mom choreographed for me and Angie and our friends Kimmy and Sharise. The end-of-year show at Mom's dance school.

Angie's pool parties. Greece …

I couldn't go on. I shut the notebook and put the pen away. The memories were making me too sad.

My stomach began to growl again. I reread the note they'd left for me, searching for clues, but of course there weren't any. I placed it on the table, as if it were a living thing, as if it would keep me company. It was my only link to the outside world.

I took out the casserole—it was made of lentils and rice and some sort of vegetable. No meat in any of the dishes, I noticed. They were probably afraid meat would spoil in this old fridge.

At least eating was something to do. The fruit salad looked tempting and turned out to be delicious. I'd never had fruit salad with whipped cream and chocolate before. Everything tasted wonderful, in fact, and I was no longer worried about the food being drugged. Nothing had happened after I ate the rice pudding.

When I'd had enough, I tried the door again. I kicked it, pounded on it, shouted, "Let me out!" until I was hoarse. There was a crack under the door and I lay down flat on the floor and tried to look out. I could see a few blades of grass and what appeared to be gravel. I never thought I'd be so grateful to see a blade of grass.

I looked at the note again. Even if it was true that I'd been brought here in an attempt at a prisoner exchange, what sort of prisoner were they trying to release? A terrorist?

That was the most likely answer. They were terrorists, and they were trying to release one of their friends. They would not hesitate to kill me if their friend was not released—and there was no chance at all that the government would yield.

They probably knew that, and merely wanted to make a point. They would kill me without hesitation as soon as it became clear that the prisoner would not be freed. In fact, even if he was freed, they'd kill me. That's what terrorists did: they killed ordinary people like me.

I began crying uncontrollably. *Why me? Why me?* I repeated over and over. The man spoke English with a British accent but also a foreign one—what kind? There was no way of knowing.

I would be executed, probably on video, maybe even tortured to death.

I had to escape. I forced myself to stop crying and focus on a plan of action. The note suggested that only one person would come—probably the man who'd brought me here. If he was unarmed, I might be able to attack him. I kept telling myself that I was in good shape, and that I knew enough karate to startle another person. All I needed was a few seconds. I'd run to the street and a car would see me.

I had to practice the moves I'd use. I regretted not going over them before I ate. Now I'd have to wait at least an hour.

I made the bed by spreading the army blanket over the mattress. Then I repacked my knapsack, even though I wouldn't be able to take it with me when I escaped. There wasn't anything irreplaceable there: guidebook, pen, sunglasses, map, tissues, deodorant, eye shadow, lip gloss, hand lotion, sunscreen, sunhat, a compact mirror, Tampax, my empty water bottle, and a silver keychain of the Greek god Pan—half goat, half man—that I'd bought at a stall.

I lifted the lid of the compact mirror. I suddenly had an overwhelming need to see my own face, and I was immensely thankful that I had this small object with me. By taking away my freedom, my hostage-takers had tried to take away my identity, turn me into an object. Seeing myself helped me reject their view of me. I wasn't a commodity to be traded; I was a real person.

I stared at my reflection for a long time. I was wearing a sleeveless purple top made of soft ribbed cotton and a necklace with a pendant Angie had made for me. I'd had my hair cut before we left for Greece; I'd asked for a choppy wash-and-wear cut that didn't need much upkeep. Thanks to Dad's Dutch ancestry, I never lost the blond hair I was born with.

It occurred to me as I gazed at the mirror that I looked stunned. I'd always felt my face wasn't interesting enough, though Angie told me that was a crazy thing to complain about, and that in fact my eyes were unusually soft, which was probably why people tended to trust me. But all I could see now in my eyes was fear and disbelief. I snapped the mirror shut.

I began to have doubts about attacking my kidnapper right away. He might just respond by killing me immediately. Or he could shoot at me as I ran. Maybe I should pretend to be docile and obedient, and then when he was no longer worried about me, I could plan an escape. As soon as I knew what the routine was, I'd know the best time to do it. *God, please help me*, I prayed.

I sat on the bed, leaned back against the wall, and looked at the three paperbacks they'd left for me: *David Copperfield*, a collection of short stories, a novel about India. I tried to read one of the stories, but I couldn't concentrate.

I decided to write Angie a letter. I opened the notebook and wrote:

> Hi Angie,
> So who would have thought our vacation would end with me being kidnapped!! Not the sort of adventure we had in mind ... Still, nothing bad has happened yet, and with a bit of luck I'll be home in a few days and we'll be laughing about it. Good thing it wasn't you, there are cockroaches here, you'd go nutso. They don't bother me, I just pretend they're the Cockroach Prince instead of the Frog Prince, though I do not

intend to catch one and kiss it in order to find out. So the food is good and you'll be happy to hear all vegetarian. Who has brought me here? That remains to be seen. Maybe the evil queen who wants to be the fairest one of all. Don't worry, I'm not losing my mind, just remembering all the fairy tales Dad used to read to me, because what's happening to me is pretty much equally unreal. Lots of love, and whatever you do, don't blame yourself, you can't control the universe. Give Pumpkin a kiss and an ear-scratch for me and tell Mom not to worry and try to keep your room in order because I can't get to you right now to help you find missing beads.

xoxoxoxxoxoxoxoxo

I tore a blank page out of the notebook and folded it into an envelope, which I addressed. For a return address I wrote "Chloe Mills, imprisoned by criminals." In the corner I drew a little stamp with the Statue of Liberty on it. I'd never really thought about its name before. Liberty: what I no longer had. What I longed for more than anything else.

I slipped the letter through the crack under the door. I did it as a kind of bleak joke, to make myself feel better.

But then I had an idea.

It occurred to me that someone might pass by the warehouse, and I wrote on another sheet of paper HELP! CALL POLICE! and slid it out as well.

But when I checked a few minutes later, the sheet had blown away. So this time I wrote TAKEN HOSTAGE IN WARE-HOUSE NEAR HERE PLEASE HELP ME, CHLOE MILLS and prayed the sheet would blow away where someone would find it. I tore out all the remaining pages in the notebook and repeated the message—the more pages out there, the better my chances.

At first it made me feel better to send out those messages for help. I prayed for a strong wind and wished they'd left me more than one notebook.

But then, suddenly, I was scared. If no one saw those pages in time to rescue me, the hostage-taker would see them when he returned. He'd be furious with me. And he'd never bring me paper again.

I wanted to take the notes back, but it was too late.

I wondered whether I should risk taking a shower. I was afraid of being in there when my captor arrived, naked and unable to hear anyone coming. But the desire to wash myself won out. I'd simply have to build a barricade.

Luckily, the door to the warehouse opened inwards.

I dragged the table to the door and set the two chairs on top of it. I positioned the chairs as precariously as possible, so that if someone came in while I was in the shower they'd both come crashing down. With a bit of luck I'd have enough time to grab my clothes and get dressed.

The shampoo on the shelf was bland and sticky, and the water was only tepid, but I was grateful for both. I felt better after my shower. Maybe everything would be okay.

The day passed in a haze of fear and boredom. I didn't have any paper left, so I wrote and doodled in the margins of my guidebook. I began *David Copperfield*—I'd seen a movie version with Daniel Radcliffe, the Harry Potter guy, and scenes came back to me as I read. At first I was discouraged because I didn't know what a *caul* was and therefore had no idea what the first page was all about, but it turned out not to matter. What came after that page was easy to understand, and it was wonderful to have a distraction from the present.

I also exercised. I did push-ups and sit-ups and practiced my karate. I was desperate for some music. If only my MP3 hadn't vanished from the *katikies* while Angie and I were away!

I nibbled on food all day. I kept wondering whether terrorists would go to all this trouble to prepare tasty meals for me. Maybe it was some sort of last meal ritual. I seemed to remember reading something about chocolates being sent to the families of women who were raped and executed by Saddam Hussein's army.

I sobbed as I ate. I wasn't the sort of person who cried, usually, and I couldn't remember the last time I'd broken down before all this happened. I was more than making up for it now.

I watched the windows darken as evening fell. Loneliness came over me like a physical illness—a haunting, hollow, desert-island feeling that was unbearable. I had no phone, no computer, no way of reaching anyone. I longed for company and at the same time I was terrified of who might come.

I was afraid to fall asleep. I piled more items on my barricade: the plate, mug, spoon, and knife, the mop and pail, the shampoo bottle, the empty food containers.

I took the fork to bed with me. If I had the guts, maybe I could poke out the terrorist's or pervert's eyes with it. I wondered why they trusted me with metal cutlery.

Eventually I dozed off, though I woke up continually during the night. I had kept the light on, and each time I woke, I was relieved to see that the barricade was still in place.

I remember dreaming about my dog Pumpkin—half poodle, half unknown. We rescued him from a shelter, and he was one of those dogs everyone fell instantly in love with. In my dream I hugged him and kissed him and cried into his fur. When I woke up my pillow was soaking wet.

Two Youths Arrested in Chloe Mills Hoax

Two 13-year-old boys from a Boston suburb were charged today with mischief for creating a bogus video of missing Chicago teenager Chloe Mills, who vanished in Greece. The boys cannot be named because of their age but have been identified on Internet blogs worldwide.

The boys' attorney, Gerard Crane, said, "They thought it would be obvious that it was a joke. They showed poor judgment and are sorry for the pain they caused."

The boys reportedly used footage of Chloe performing gymnastics routines along with sophisticated animation and live-action technology to create the impression that the teenager was being stabbed to death. The boys posted the homemade video on YouTube, identifying themselves as "Al Qaeda Super Warriors." The video was removed almost immediately and directed to the appropriate security officials.

The video has brought the disappearance of Chloe further into the spotlight as police continue to investigate.

Allegra Mills, Chloe's mother, said she will not be pressing charges. Speaking from an Athens hotel, she told reporters: "I hope they will be more responsible in the future." Though near tears, Ms. Mills added that she is trying to remain optimistic about her daughter's fate.

POST REPORT

CHAPTER 6

Waking up in the warehouse, imprisoned and alone, I felt more miserable than afraid. Maybe I was still too bleary to be afraid.

I dragged myself to the little bathroom, washed up, and forced myself to exercise. I kept wanting to throw myself on the bed in despair, but I knew I had to concentrate on the task of overcoming my captor and not let misery weaken me.

I was on the bed reading *David Copperfield* when I heard a sound on the other side of the door, then a knock.

I jumped up on the bed, clutching the fork in my hand. My heart began thumping against my chest.

Then I remembered that I was supposed to pretend to be cooperative, and take the terrorist or pervert or whatever he was by surprise, so I quickly hid the fork under the blanket. The important thing was to stay in control, I told myself, but my heart was pounding so hard I was afraid something inside me would tear.

The door opened and the barricade came crashing down. The mug broke into several pieces.

A tall man wearing black jeans and a long-sleeved white shirt, and carrying several plastic bags, entered the warehouse. My SOS messages and the letter to Angie were tucked under his arm.

I assumed he was the man who had brought me here. His movements and appearance matched the casual voice I'd heard, and I had caught a glimpse of his black jeans through my blindfold.

It was a shock, seeing him now. I realized I'd created a picture of him in my mind, and though the picture went in and out of focus, and details kept changing, I'd imagined him having shaggy black hair, a Che Guevara cap, a Che Guevara beard, olive-brown skin, a stocky build. When he retied my blindfold, I imagined large, muscular hands.

But he didn't look anything like that. The only thing I was right about was his height, which I'd been able to estimate from the sound of his voice and where it came from. I'd guessed that he was close to six feet—nearly eight inches taller than me—and I was right.

I was also right about his black or nearly black hair, but it was on the short side, and he was clean-shaven. He was slender rather than stocky and burly, and his long hands made me think of Angie's poster of *Venus and Mars*.

What most stood out for me, though, was how ordinary he looked. He could have been someone you passed on the street or sat next to on the bus. He didn't look mad or cruel. In fact, I had to admit that he was good-looking. It confused and upset me, to register that he was attractive. Not that I wanted him to be scarily hideous, but finding him attractive seemed crazy and somehow wrong.

But the real shock was what a relief it was for me to see another human being. I'd been deprived of company for only a short time, but I was already hungry for it. Hungry to know I wasn't alone in the world—even if the person I was seeing was not only a stranger but was the one responsible for how alone I was.

I was shocked by my own desperation, by the intensity of my need. It seemed like a great bonus, that I was allowed to see my captor, and I resented my gratitude.

Then I remembered that he was probably a terrorist and that he could kill me at any moment. It didn't matter what he looked like; the only thing that mattered was whether I'd survive.

He stared at the barrier I'd set up for a few seconds, and then he stared at me. I was standing on the bed with my back to the wall, and I must have looked terrified, but he didn't betray any reaction to the barricade or to my fear. He locked the door on the inside with a combination lock. Then he moved the table and chairs back to the center of the room and began to empty the plastic bags. His face was expressionless.

I watched him put away the items he'd brought: more plates, a bottle of wine, two wine glasses, dishwashing detergent, instant coffee, tea bags in a jar, mint leaves in a jar, sugar, more cutlery, and more food. He had also brought a hot plate, a small pot, a few more books, two more empty notebooks, and another ballpoint pen.

To my surprise, he placed the books and pen and notebooks on the bed.

He said, "This is on condition that you stop slipping notes under the door. There's no one around here anyhow. But if you persist, I'll have to confiscate the paper."

I was right: it was the same man. I recognized his voice. *Persist … confiscate*—he used such strange, formal English. As if we were in a classroom.

"I promise," I managed to say. At least he wasn't planning to kill me right away. He wouldn't have brought all those things, he wouldn't be giving me notebooks.

He began collecting the shards of the broken mug. Then he took the first notebook, which I'd left on the floor by my bed, sat down at the table, and matched the messages to the missing pages. He seemed satisfied that he had them all. He returned the letter to me without reading it.

"Are you going to kill me?" I asked. I didn't know what I was going to say until I spoke, and I didn't know that my voice would sound so shaky.

He looked at me for a few seconds and then said, "No."

"What sort of prisoner are you asking for?" I asked, trying to steady myself. What I meant, of course, was, *What are your politics?*

But all he said was, "An innocent one." His composed voice made him seem less threatening, but also very distant, and the relief I'd felt at seeing another person was quickly vanishing.

"Can't you just hire a better lawyer?"

"That's already been tried."

"What if you don't get the prisoner? Will you kill me then?"

"No."

"How can I believe you?"

"We'll let you go whether the attempt works or not."

"But now I know what you look like," I said, panicking again. My fear was like sea waves, receding for a few seconds, then surging through me with renewed force.

"There are over six billion people on the planet. I'm sure many of them look like me."

"I guess it's good you don't have six fingers," I said, trying to ride the wave.

"I'm glad you're keeping your sense of humor," he said. "Would you like some wine?"

He stared at me and I stared back. It was as if we were two predatory animals, sizing each other up in some life-and-death contest. "How come you trust me with a glass bottle?" I asked.

"I like to live dangerously," he said, and I felt ridiculous. Now that he was here, a real live person rather than an imagined figure, the possibility of breaking a glass bottle over his head or attacking him with a fork seemed as farfetched as digging my way out of this place with a spoon.

In any case, the door was locked with a combination lock. Very clever! I couldn't escape, even if I knocked him out.

"Why are you giving me this food, and the wine?"

"There's no reason for you to suffer more than necessary."

"Then let me go!"

"Freeing my friend is more important."

"Are you terrorists?" I asked recklessly.

"No. Not terrorists and not any other euphemisms that are used."

Euphemisms ... he was smart. That was a good thing— you could reason with a smart person, you could make them see things from different angles. On the other hand, a person could easily be intelligent and cruel; the most sadistic girl in our school, Rik, was a top honor student. "I thought ..." I muttered.

"Yes, it's the obvious conclusion to draw these days. But no, I'm not a terrorist of any kind."

"But if you were ... I mean ... would you admit it— would you use that word, I mean, does anyone say, 'I'm a terrorist'?"

"What I mean is that I don't believe in killing civilians to make some point."

Civilians. Wasn't that something a military person would say? Ordinary people didn't divide the world into civilians and non-civilians. "Are you British?" I asked.

"The less you know about me, the better for everyone." Since I had not answered his question about the wine, he opened the bottle and filled the two glasses.

"I don't know what to do, I don't know what to think," I said frantically. It made no sense to turn to him for direction, but there was no one else.

"It will be better for everyone if you accept the situation. We can both try to make the best of it."

"I don't seem to have much choice! Does my mother know I'm okay?"

"Yes."

"Can I write to her?"

"Yes, but only a few sentences."

"You won't get what you're asking for. I'm not important enough. If you'd kidnapped someone from the government, that might work. But no one cares about me. What a stupid idea!" I was very angry suddenly.

"You may be right," he said in the same even voice. He didn't seem to care whether I was angry. He didn't appear to be at all violent or aggressive. But what he'd done—abducting me, holding me here—these things *were* aggressive. His calm demeanor was only a facade.

He arranged the food he'd brought on the table.

"Who prepared all this?"

"I did."

"You cooked it yourself?"

"Yes."

"Where did you learn to cook?"

"I picked it up."

"Are you vegetarian? My friend Angie is."

"If there's something specific you want, let me know."

"What's your name? I mean … you can give me a fake name."

"I'd rather not."

"I'm Chloe," I said. "But you know that."

"Yes."

"Poor Angie. She's going to blame herself. You have no idea how much anguish you're causing. To my mother … and everyone. Only Mom's dad won't know. He has Alzheimer's."

He didn't answer. He served himself and began to eat. He'd brought the same sort of food: dips, salads. There were some cheese and spinach pastries too, and peach pie and vanilla pudding and a loaf of homemade bread.

I sat down at the table but I didn't join him.

"Why should I eat with you?" I said. "You're not my friend. Did you threaten to kill me?"

"Yes."

"But it's just a bluff."

"Yes."

"Or you might be lying to me, so I won't panic. You might shoot me and film it on video, like they do in Iraq."

"I'm not going to shoot you. And we are not in Iraq."

"Well, that's one country down, a hundred and ninety to go. Though I guess I can rule out Iceland too." I realized I was chatting with him as if we were in geography class and he wouldn't give me the answer to question B. It was loneliness.

He didn't smile, but he seemed amused—I could tell by his shoulders, somehow, and by the slight tilt of his head. Maybe he was amused by my practical side, the side Angie sometimes found so annoying.

"We must be near the equator," I said, leaning back in the chair. "Or you wouldn't have installed an air-conditioner."

"Yes, you can also rule out Greenland," he said, without smiling. I was somewhat disconcerted by how expressionless and immobile his face was. It could have been scary, but his eyes at least were clever and full of life. He looked at me intently, as if he were trying to see me as clearly as possible, or maybe as if he already saw me more clearly than I supposed.

"I guess I have to believe you. I guess I want to believe you. You don't look like the type to shoot an innocent person, but looks can be deceiving."

"That's true."

"If you kill me, will you do it fast?"

"I told you, no one is going to kill you."

"I don't want to die."

"Most people don't want to die."

"I've only just started my life."

"Yes."

"But I've seen you," I repeated.

"Brown hair, brown eyes, six-foot-two—that will narrow it down," he said.

"If you'd kidnapped my friend Angie, she'd be able to draw you."

"That would be bad luck."

I took a sip of wine and studied his face. Nothing about him seemed desperate or wild. He appeared to be about twenty-seven or twenty-eight. His eyes weren't brown, as he'd said, but it was hard to tell what color they were. I tried not to relate to his good looks. It seemed to me dangerous to even notice that he was attractive; I didn't want anything like that to cloud my vision or affect my judgment.

He stared at me in a way I wasn't used to, but I knew that might have more to do with culture than with personal idiosyncrasy. I'd noticed that in Greece people looked at the person they were addressing more directly than we did. I was interested in things like that—I even thought I might study anthropology when I went to university.

Of course, maybe he wasn't Greek at all. I was never much good at guessing anyone's race or background.

"You're a very serious sort of person," I said.

He looked at me but didn't answer for a change. I didn't avoid his gaze. I looked right back at him.

"Your idea won't work, you know. If the government gave in, everyone would try it. Everyone would take hostages, it would get completely out of control. Our prisons would empty out within weeks!"

"You have a point," he said, and I wondered whether he was humoring me. It was impossible to tell from his tone of voice.

"What you're doing isn't right. I've never done anything to you. Why would you make me suffer like this?"

"You're right, it's not fair to you."

"Well, I'm glad I'm not a sex slave at least. I thought some pervert may have hired you to kidnap me … You're not interested in me that way either," I said. It was a disguised question, of course. I needed confirmation.

"No," he said. "You don't have to worry about that."

I looked down and shuffled my feet under the table. I felt embarrassed, but I was glad I'd asked.

"One hour before you need hot water, turn on the boiler. It shuts automatically, so you need to switch it on each time."

"I didn't see any boiler."

"It's next to the shower."

"Okay."

"If you need anything, let me know."

"I guess I'm lucky, relatively speaking. I mean, you could have been horrible. But you seem nice, actually. Apart from this very stupid idea of yours." I was no longer afraid of him. It was obvious he wasn't going to hurt me, no matter what I said. If he was going to kill me, it would be because of what he'd decided, not because of anything I said or did.

He went on eating, and in spite of my resolution not to join him, I helped myself to a cheese and spinach pastry.

"I don't need so much food," I said.

"I wasn't sure what you liked."

"Did you give a deadline?"

"Yes, one month."

His answer jolted me back to reality. It was easy to get drawn into his casual style, his informal conversation. Easy to slip into semi-denial and pretend that we were friends, because that was so much more bearable than the truth. I felt cold suddenly, and I shivered. A month! How would I survive?

"Will you extend it if you don't get your prisoner back by then?" I asked.

"Yes."

"You're in charge of my life now."

I waited for him to sip the wine before I drank from my glass. "You're my food taster," I said. "This way I know it's not spiked."

"I'm sorry you're having all these fears," he said.

"Not sorry enough," I mumbled.

He tilted his head, and I felt again that he was amused.

When he'd finished eating, he washed his dishes in the bathroom sink and carried them back to the table. He said, "I brought you a hot plate in case you want tea. It needs to be unplugged when you're not using it."

"Thank you," I said without thinking and immediately felt stupid. Why was I thanking my jailer? But he seemed not to have heard and I wondered whether I'd actually spoken or just thought I had.

He reached into one of the plastic bags, pulled out a large piece of black cloth, and slung it over the saloon doors. It reached the floor, and I wondered whether he was trying to provide me with more privacy. But I was on the wrong track. He took a camera out of his pocket—my camera.

"I need a photo of you, please. If you could sit in front of the door."

"And if I refuse?" I asked, just to see what he'd say.

"No pizza."

This time his flippancy made me angry. It was as if he thought this was all some sort of game. As if he had no idea how much suffering he was causing my mom and grandparents, or how much he'd terrified me. A huge wave of hatred came over me, and I wanted to punch him. I forced myself not to give in to my fury. I sat cross-legged on the floor, with the black cloth behind me.

"Just sit up a little, please, maybe on your knees—you're too low."

Trying to control my voice, I asked, "Is this photo for the newspapers?"

"Yes."

"Can you take a few, so I can choose the best one?" I didn't want him to send out a photo that looked too sad.

I wanted Mom to know that I was all right, and I did my best to smile into the camera.

"Don't smile, please."

Not being allowed to smile made me even angrier, if that was possible. I took a deep breath, shut my eyes for a second, and concentrated on the message I wanted to send Mom and my friends. I wanted to say so much through the photo—tell Mom I loved her, tell everyone not to worry.

He took five shots and handed me the camera. I looked at all the photos and chose the one that seemed least frightened. I had tried not to look scared at all, but I didn't succeed.

"I'm probably the first kidnapped person in history who got to choose her photo," I said.

"While I'm gone, you can make a list of things you need. Is there anything urgent, before I go?"

The thought of being left alone again was suddenly frightening. "Don't go yet. I don't like being alone here."

He considered for a moment. Then he said, "I'll return in a minute."

He undid the combination lock and stepped out. He shut the door, but I noticed that he didn't lock it. I could hardly believe it—this was my chance. I hadn't had to plan it at all.

Chloe Mills Abducted by Terrorists

The U.S. Embassy in Greece has been contacted by a party claiming to be holding Chloe Mills, the Chicago high school student who disappeared in August. An embassy spokesperson said the evidence that the group is holding Chloe is "convincing" and that a "list of demands" was put forth, but declined to elaborate.

Chloe's mother, Allegra Mills, said, "I'm relieved to know she's alive and I know the police are doing everything they can. Please, everyone, pray for Chloe in your way." Ms. Mills, a widow, is in Greece in order to follow the investigation into her daughter's disappearance.

See p. B1 for the full story.

POST REPORT

CHAPTER 7

I threw my body against the door and began to run. There was a tall aluminum fence on my right and a forest straight ahead, only twenty feet or so from the door. I dashed toward it and began weaving as fast as I could through the trees.

I heard the man running behind me. The ground was uneven and branches kept getting in my way and slowing me down. I hadn't gone very far when he grabbed my arm.

I tried to kick him, but he moved aside in time. I tried again, this time using my arms as well. To my disappointment, he knew as much karate as I did, probably more. And he was stronger. In a few seconds he had maneuvered me so that I was lying on the ground on my stomach, the side of my face flat against the earth and dry grass. He had my arms in a clasp behind me.

"Let's go back," he said evenly, as though we'd gone out for a pleasant stroll together.

He let go and I sat up, breathing heavily, my heart pounding. "I think I twisted my ankle," I lied, just to buy time.

He saw right through me, of course. He said, "If your ankle hurts you can lean on me."

I wondered why he wasn't dragging me back. Maybe he was afraid of attracting attention, in case someone saw us.

"I need to catch my breath," I said, still hoping to buy time, or at least enjoy the cool forest air for a few more seconds. Maybe I'd be lucky and someone would show up.

"No," he said. "We have to go back."

I sighed and got up. At least I knew now that he wasn't violent. He could have hurt me when we fought, but he didn't. Even when he twisted my arm behind my back, it was only to hold me down.

"Small mercies," I mumbled, not expecting him to understand or even hear me.

But he said, "The approach of an optimist."

As we came out of the forest I tried to take in as much as I could of my surroundings. The tall aluminum fence, now on my left, extended from the warehouse to the forest and blocked the view on that side completely. On the other side, facing the fence, was the back wall of what seemed to be another massive warehouse. A second fence created a narrow alley between the two buildings. I wondered whether we were in some sort of industrial park or compound.

My mistake had been to run in the direction of the forest. I decided to make a second dash for it. This time I'd run down the alley toward the entrance of the compound. There was bound to be a road at the end of it.

But he anticipated my move. He caught me at once, slung me over his shoulder, and carried me back to the warehouse. I felt small and insignificant on his shoulder. I pounded his back and yelled, "Help! Help me!" But there was no one around. He stepped into the warehouse and let me down.

I was sure he'd leave now. He went out and locked the door this time. But after a few seconds he returned with a briefcase.

"I hate this. I hate you," I blurted out. I regretted it right away—I couldn't afford to alienate the person who was in charge of my food, my conditions, my life.

But he replied evenly, "No one likes to be imprisoned."

I thought again of the Patty Hearst movie. I was luckier than her—so far, at least. I wasn't blindfolded in a small closet with people hammering on the walls; a deluded egomaniac wasn't trying to convert and seduce me.

"I saw a movie about Patty Hearst once," I said. "On late-night TV. Have you seen it?"

"I saw a documentary about her."

"No, this was a real movie."

"I'm not familiar with it."

"At least I'm not getting brainwashed."

He didn't answer. He sat at the table, unlocked his brief-case, and took out several books. He pulled the standing lamp closer to the table and began to read and make notes. He seemed to be doing research or writing an essay. As far as I could see, the books were in English, but I couldn't make out any of the titles.

I wondered whether he was a university student, and whether during the day he attended classes. No one would know he was a hostage-taker—like students who went to Ivy League universities during the day and worked as call girls at night. I sat down on the bed and hugged my knees.

"It's a warm evening," I said.

He looked up at me. "Yes, dusk is my favorite time of day."

I felt he was offering me a gift by making this personal comment, but the gift made me resentful. Why should I be grateful to him for being friendly? He had locked me up in a warehouse, he was traumatizing my poor mother, he had terrified me.

It bothered me that I had to remind myself who he was. He kept trying to make me forget.

Maybe he wasn't all that different from Patty Hearst's abductors after all. Maybe his methods were just more subtle. First step: make the kidnapped person forget that what you've done is wrong.

Well, I wasn't going to forget. Nor was I going to get brainwashed. No one could change who I was and what I believed in. At least I had that.

"How can you send the photo to the press? They'll track down the computer. Oh! Why did I tell you that!"

He looked up. "Yes, you should have kept that to yourself," he said, teasing me.

I was too angry to answer. I opened one of the new notebooks and wrote Mom a letter:

Dear Mom, I'm okay. I have everything I need and I'm being treated well so don't worry. I have a shower and hot water, and lots of food. I'm not allowed to say anything about the people who took me hostage, but I have books and anything else I want, and I'll try to spend the time productively. I love you. Give Pumpkin a big hug and don't worry because as you always say, everything will work out. Please check the vet calendar for Pumpkin's shots. Love to Oma and Opa and all my friends and tell Angie it wasn't her fault. Don't worry! I love you and miss you, Chloe.

I tore out the page and handed it to my hostage-taker.

"It's mostly okay," he said. "Just take out the information about the food and the books, and the words *and anything else I want*. Also take out that you're going to spend the time usefully. You can keep everything else."

"You want people to think I'm suffering."

"Yes."

I didn't think I could be any angrier than I already was, but my rage rose to a whole new level. I was furious that I had to do what he told me to, furious that he wanted to hurt my mom, furious that I couldn't reassure her. I was so angry my hand began to shake.

I was afraid that if my hand shook, Mom would think I was writing at gunpoint or that I was lying in order to make her feel better.

"I'm too angry to write steadily," I said.

"It's better for you, too, not to give more information. No one would believe you anyhow. It's more credible if you keep it simple."

I didn't say anything, though I had to admit he had a point. I took a few breaths, focused on mind control, and rewrote the letter. I changed the part he told me to change. I wrote instead: *I'm not allowed to say anything about the people who took me hostage, but I'm all right.*

"Much better," he said. He slid the letter into his brief-case and continued working.

I noticed that he was wearing a watch on his right wrist, and I decided to ask for my watch back, or for a clock. Knowing what time it was would help me orient myself. I wanted to ask him why he took away my watch in the first place, but I was afraid that if I made a nuisance of myself he'd leave.

Instead, I worked on my list. I didn't know how many things to ask for. The group he belonged to obviously had a lot of money, but if I asked for too much, I wouldn't get what I most wanted.

I finally narrowed my list down to the things I needed in order to keep my sanity.

clock or watch
mat for exercising (two or three if possible)
magazines and newspapers—all kinds
music—all kinds
DVD player or laptop and movies
tennis racket and ball
hairbrush
woman's razor and foam OR electric
hand soap for sensitive skin
skin lotion
box of tissues
decent shampoo and conditioner
panties (2) and pair of cotton socks

nail file
book for learning Italian or German
more towels
flip-flops or slippers
crossword puzzles, dictionary, playing cards

I'd never been interested in crossword puzzles, but I fig-
ured it would be something to do. I wasn't really into cards
either. I only knew one version of solitaire, but maybe I could
play poker or blackjack with my hostage-taker. I had to take
Italian or German in my last year, so I could try to get a head
start on that. At least I'd have the illusion that I'd be going
home eventually.

In fact I no longer believed that I'd be killed for the simple
reason that I couldn't maintain that degree of fear. It was too
hard. I had to believe that I'd make it through this.

When I finished the list, I made a calendar. I wasn't sure
whether it was Wednesday or Thursday, but I took a guess and
went from there.

I shut the notebook and leaned back against the wall.
I would have done anything for a phone—preferably an
iPhone. It was agony not to be able to email or text or talk to
somebody. It was the worst part of my situation, apart from
not knowing my future.

I watched my hostage-taker as he worked. He was reading several books at once, looking for passages, and making
notes. I wondered what the topic was. Politics, probably. How
to take hostages …

I tried to read too, but I couldn't concentrate. It was hard, sitting there in the spooky silence, not saying a word. Finally I asked, "Are you looking up recipes?"

He looked at me and tilted his head, but his expression didn't change. He checked his watch, then he pressed his eyes with the palms of his hands. "I have to go now," he said. "I'll be back tomorrow evening."

"I guess hostage-taking is tiring."

He didn't answer. He put his books and papers away and clicked his briefcase shut.

I handed him my list.

"I'll see what I can manage," he said, looking it over.

"Why did you take my watch?"

"So you wouldn't know how much time had passed."

I wondered why he was being so open with me. Maybe it was a strategy. Maybe everything he did was a strategy: the joking, the good food, the wine.

"Your eyes aren't exactly brown," I said, trying to keep him from leaving.

He pretended not to hear me. Without saying goodbye, he undid the combination lock and left. I suddenly remembered that I'd forgotten to ask for pajamas, and I pounded on the door and called out to him, but it was too late. He was gone.

Angie Shaw Thanks for all the comments, everyone. It really helps to know so many people are supporting Chloe. Don't forget to join the Free Chloe Campaign—there's a fundraiser in the works and we need all the help we can get spreading the word. It's so hard not to know anything about what's happening to her, where she is, how they're treating her, the imagination starts going and there's no end to it. I lie in bed awake thinking thinking thinking, feeling so helpless. Going over the last day, which is really pointless but I can't help it. Wishing I'd gone with her … Anyhow, as far as the demands, nothing is really confirmed, but it seems they, I mean the guys holding Chloe (it freaks me out to call them terrorists)—anyhow, it seems they have a thing against this public prosecutor Lawrence "the horror" Mayfair-Horrick, known to be a bigot, very controversial. According to rumors they want two releases, two retrials, nine parole reviews, and twenty-one prisoner transfers—all are guys this Mayfair-Horrick person prosecuted. Meanwhile he's recovering from bypass surgery after consuming nothing but pork, bacon, and ham since he was around three months old. Says he doesn't care less what the gov't does. PLEASE BE OK CHLOE.

32 minutes ago   Comment   Like   Wall-to-wall

Jeanette Persky Why aren't we getting all the details???

28 minutes ago   Comment   Like   Wall-to-wall

Matthias Santiago They (the guys on top) are probably having frantic meetings about what to do. If it was a pure exchange it would be simpler, there's a policy and they'd just stick to it and say no way josé, especially if the prisoner's a lifer or on death row. But this is more complicated, harder to say no and a lot of pressure from all sorts of lobby groups and people who hate this Mayfair-Horrick guy regardless. The question is: can the AG review the cases and file a request with the court of appeal if the appeal time limit has passed? Ditto for parole review. So that might be a problem, I don't know if it's written in stone. That's why I think what the Chloe campaign is doing is good—hire lawyers and see if it can all be done quasi-legitimately to start off with.

15 minutes ago   Comment   Like   Wall-to-wall

 Angie Shaw The main thing is not to forget about her! I'm so glad she's still in the news—though some of those tabloids, have you seen them??? There is NO WAY they can know that Chloe's been tortured or anything else!! She sounded okay in her letter, I think she's okay. I notice my art has changed completely btw, in Greece it was all stone and sand and light and now there's this wild, slashing thing going on. Don't worry it's just on canvas! I love you all, your support is so amazing. We'll have a huge party when she gets back—it will happen. How about this for our slogan—"Chloe Come Home"? I'll post it on the Free Chloe Campaign site and ask for votes. What do you think?

2 minutes ago   Comment   Like   Wall-to-wall

CHAPTER 8

I didn't fall asleep right away. I wondered whether he was lying about everything. I thought about his expressionless face, his cool and casual voice. His impassivity was not entirely reassuring: he didn't give anything away. He may have been putting on an act for me, pretending to be considerate and concerned. *Sorry for the inconvenience!* Yes, sorry for terrorizing you and your family and friends. Sorry for locking you up. Sorry for threatening to kill you and making you think you were a sex slave. Sorry.

Could I rely on the fact that he didn't look or act like an insane criminal? People who seemed polite and harmless sometimes ended up being serial killers—and after all, he'd done all this. He'd put me here. Not only that: he'd done it in a very careful and calculated way. Every detail had been planned in advance. He was extremely intelligent, and that also meant that he could be an excellent liar.

I finally sank into a deep, dreamless sleep, and I woke up feeling a little better. I decided to make the best of the situation, find a way to make it bearable.

I turned on the boiler and had a shower. The hot water was soothing, and I even sang to myself—I was desperate for music.

After the shower I exercised. I revived some old gymnastics moves and then moved on to aerobics. I didn't bother with karate.

I'd finished exercising and was trying to decide whether

to have a second bowl of vanilla pudding when there was a loud pounding on the door.

I froze. The pounding scared me. It didn't sound like the man from the day before. He wouldn't pound on the door, he'd knock. Besides, he wasn't due back until evening. There were a few more loud bangs and then I heard a terrifying male voice: "I am coming in. Put on your blindfold or I'll shoot you."

"Wait! Wait!" I called out. I was right, it had all been a lie. It had all been an act. How could I have let myself be taken in?

I looked around frantically for the blindfold. Then I remembered that I'd put it inside my knapsack. I emptied the knapsack on the bed and desperately rummaged through everything, but it wasn't there. The hammering on the door continued, and my heart seemed to be hammering just as hard. I felt around inside the knapsack and to my relief I found the blindfold at the very bottom. Everything seemed to be taking ten times longer than it would normally and my fingers were so stiff I could barely make a knot. I wondered whether this was the end for me. Or worse.

"Okay!" I said as loudly as I could without sounding aggressive. I didn't want to make the man angrier than he already was.

The door flew open and I heard someone charging into the warehouse. I could see his shoes through my blindfold— old, dirty sneakers with laces.

"American whore," he said in a hollow, raspy voice that sounded as if he'd been up for several nights drinking, and was possibly still drunk, though I didn't smell any alcohol. He had an accent, but it was different from the other man's.

I knew at once that I was in trouble. I'd been right, they were terrorists. They hated me, and they were going to kill me, though maybe not right away. Maybe they would torture me first.

I began to sob hysterically, though I tried to control myself. I wanted to be in control so I could at least make an effort to overcome him. Should I rip off my blindfold and try my karate on him? Maybe he wasn't as good at fighting as the other man.

But I was too frightened to do anything and a second later it was too late. My wrists were tied behind my back. "Please," I said. "I haven't done anything. I'm not even old enough to vote," I added inanely, as if I could reason with him.

How to have fun with a hostage: Bring hostage to knees. Dunk her head in a pail of water until she's convinced she's drowning. Let up for air. Repeat as often as desired, until sadistic urges subside. Leave hostage lying on floor. Don't forget to kick the pail, so the water spills everywhere.

I would like to forget what happened, or at least for the memory to fade, but instead I can recall every tiny detail in its exact sequence, as if my brain had turned into some kind of video recorder. The only thing I can't know is how long he was there—was it ten minutes? Half an hour? An hour? Everything else, everything I thought and felt, is weirdly vivid. I remember the smell of the metal pail, the piercing pain of its rusty edges on my throat, my eyes burning under the soaking blindfold.

I was sure I was going to die. I wanted to talk, to answer

the man's hollow shouts and accusations, to explain things to him, but I couldn't even breathe. It was as if ten different types of pain had invaded me. The worst was a blackout pain at the back of my eyes. I couldn't help swallowing the dirty water, which tasted of some horrible cleanser, and I thought, *If I don't die of drowning I'll die of poisoning.*

For some reason I remembered some TV show about sadistic parents who dunked their kid's head in the sink as a punishment. And about how sadists justify themselves. How all sadists justify themselves in the same way. No matter what people do, no matter how horrible it is, they can invent a reason—or several reasons—to explain why it's right and good to do what they did. I even had a flash of the five major justifications that had appeared on the screen in point form. *I had no choice. They deserved it. Everyone does it. I'm a hero for doing what I believe in.* I couldn't remember the fifth one.

The man was weak. I could tell by the way he pushed me that he was physically weak, even frail. Had I not panicked, had I taken off my blindfold and rushed at him, I would have been able to knock him out, even if he had a weapon. I could have disarmed him if I'd acted fast. But by the time I realized he was weak, whether naturally or because he was drunk or on drugs, I was even weaker than him. Every bit of energy I had was concentrated on trying to breathe.

He had his fun and then he left. I was alive after all, but maybe that was only because he wasn't through. Maybe he'd be back to finish the job later.

I lay on the wet floor, unable to move. I was coughing and

gasping and my head felt as if it had smashed into a hard object. I lifted the wet blindfold from my eyes and tried to get up so I could shower, but the room began to spin and I passed out instead.

I don't know how long I lay there. At some point I became aware of warm air in my mouth, and I began to cough.

I was wrapped in the army blanket and my feet were raised on a pillow. The man from the day before was blowing air into my lungs.

I watched myself from a great distance. I felt completely detached, as if nothing could possibly affect me.

I became aware that my fingers were frozen stiff. I couldn't move them at all. But it didn't worry me. Nothing did.

"I'm hot," I said, trying to pull away from the blanket.

"It's better if you stay warm."

"I'm too hot."

He loosened the blanket. "Do you think you can drink some water?"

"I can't move my hands."

"I'll hold the bottle for you." He held my head up slightly with one hand and with the other he brought the water bottle to my mouth. Then he held my wrist and checked my pulse.

"I want to go home," I said. "I want my mom. Mommy, Mommy." I knew I sounded like a small child but that was exactly how I felt—small and helpless.

"It's not a good idea to move. You'll pass out again." I saw now that he was furious. I felt it in his body and I heard it in his voice, though he was trying to conceal it.

I became aware of an unpleasant smell and I realized, to my horror, that the smell was coming from me. I'd wet my pants.

"I have to wash. I have to wash," I said. Hearing the frantic pitch of my own voice made me realize that I was on the brink of hysteria.

"Please try to relax. It would be better to wait."

"No, I need to wash," I insisted. "I need to wash now."

"I can do it for you if you allow me."

Allow—as if I had a choice. But I only nodded. It was too much effort to speak.

He wet a towel and wiped my face. Then, without warning, I threw up on everything—the floor, his arm, the blanket. I had just enough time to twist sideways. It was beyond horrible.

"It's okay," he said. He was very upset. He placed his hand on my forehead, as if checking for fever. It felt so good, having that reassurance, and he must have sensed how consoling it was for me because he left his hand there longer than he needed to. Almost instinctively he drew my hair back and I felt he wanted to stroke my hair to soothe me, but he stopped himself.

I shut my eyes as he cleaned the mess. I didn't care at all about being exposed in front of him. I was in too much pain to care, and too detached. If anything, I hoped he was disgusted. I hoped he was sickened and disgusted and embarrassed.

But probably neither of us cared. There were new rules in place now.

My throat was burning, and I remembered that I'd swallowed cleanser. "I've been poisoned, I've been poisoned!"

I began to scream.

"Please try to calm down."

"There was cleanser in the water. In the pail. And I swallowed it."

"It was only dishwashing soap in there, and I don't think all that much. You'll be okay." I felt him trying to control his anger as he spoke. He wasn't steady or calm now.

I wanted to believe him. I shut my eyes and moaned. "I can't move my hands," I said.

He began to massage my fingers. I felt a great wave of misery coming over him, replacing the anger.

The massage worked. One by one, my fingers relaxed. "I'm ready for bed now," I muttered. "I need to get these jeans off." I began to pull at the jeans, but they clung to my legs. "Help me, please," I said. I pushed my jeans and panties off under the blanket while he pulled at the legs. "Okay, I'm ready for bed," I told him.

"I'll carry you," he said.

The blanket fell off as he lifted me. I didn't care. I was very dizzy and I held on to him. I felt his rage returning as he carried me to the mattress.

I must have passed out again. When I woke up my head was throbbing.

"Bathroom," I groaned.

"I'll give you a hand. Maybe you'd like to put on the skirt while your jeans dry?"

I shook my head. There wasn't time, and I didn't have the energy. He wrapped the sheet around me, helped me to the bathroom and left me there. My stomach was grinding away; I had cramps, nausea—I was a mess. I noticed my jeans hanging on the shower rod.

When I was back in bed, he said, "You need to keep drinking. Can you manage some more water?"

I shut my eyes and saw myself hurtling through a tunnel, and at the end of the tunnel was the brutal man, waiting for me.

"My head hurts," I moaned.

"Did you hit your head against something?"

"Yes, against the heart of darkness, ha ha."

He took my wrist and felt my pulse again. He said, "You're better now. Your color is returning, your pulse rate is almost normal. You're over the worst, I think. Can you drink a little?"

"My throat hurts."

He looked straight at me and said, "This wasn't supposed to happen. It will never happen again."

A strange thing happened then. I'd heard about people reliving experiences and I thought it meant that you recall the experience vividly. But it isn't like that. It's more like a waking dream. You think, feel, and react exactly as you did during the event, as if the event was actually recurring.

Without warning I sat up as if I'd been startled and began alternately shrieking and whimpering. I was sure I was going to die, I choked and retched and pleaded, I wasn't in the present at all. Then it was over, and I was aware that my hostage-taker was kneeling behind me with his arms clasped around my waist.

"Do you want to lie down?" he asked, letting go of me.

"My throat hurts," I said. I felt humiliated and ashamed, and I wanted to forget what had just happened.

"I'll make tea." He boiled water on the hot plate and made me sweet tea. I watched him without really understanding what he was doing.

"I don't know what that was all about," I mumbled when he handed me the mug. I didn't mind that he'd seen me vomit, or that he'd had to wash my urine-soaked jeans, but I was embarrassed that I'd lost control in front of him.

"You're very strong," he replied. "Everyone reacts that way. You're not an exception."

How would you know? I wanted to say. But I was too afraid of him. I could no longer trust him not to hurt me, even if he was being nice now. Who knew what he was capable of, what kind of double personality he had?

A dreadful thought came to me. *Everyone reacts that way*—did he mean all the other girls he'd brought to this warehouse? What if the entire prisoner exchange story was invented, what if he was nothing more than a psychotic kidnapper, playacting a role to disguise his real intention?

Maybe he was delusional, like people who think they're Napoleon—maybe he thought he was some kind of revolutionary hero, and he was lying about contacting the media. The other guy had to be working for him—how could he not be? Someone gave him the key. Someone who knew what he was like.

"How do you know everyone reacts that way?" I asked, trying to hide my fear.

"It's common knowledge," he said. "I've never taken anyone hostage before, if that's what you're wondering. There are no skeletons buried in the backyard."

I was suddenly too tired to think. The hot, sweet tea made me drowsy and I wondered vaguely if it was drugged. I didn't care if it was. I wanted to sleep. "Why were my fingers stiff like that?" I asked.

"Just stress. How do you feel?"

"Like a house landed on my head," I said, my voice barely audible. "Even though I was the good witch."

"I'll get you some painkillers."

"Your friend. Your friend," I said, panicking at the thought of being left alone.

"I can promise you nothing like this will happen again. I know it's impossible for you to trust me now. But I don't even know what went on. And it would help me if you told me, so I can get you what you need."

I didn't answer. I was too wiped out. Instead I took his hand and held it.

I don't know why I took his hand. I think I was just desperate. Desperate to have a friend, desperate to believe him. I knew now that I was on the brink of real disaster and that he was the only one standing between me and that disaster. I could have been left on the floor to die. Instead I was in bed drinking tea.

He pulled his hand away and said, "I think you have a fever. I'll go get something to bring it down and for your stomach. I'll return in an hour or so. No one else will come—

I'm putting the combination lock on the outside."

"I want my teddy bear," I whispered. I was growing more confused by the minute, and it really did seem to me that he could go upstairs and fetch me my old teddy bear.

"I'll be back soon."

www.free-chloe.org

Free Chloe

Search this site

home | contact | about us | about Chloe | updates | blog

This is a letter to the people who are holding my daughter, Chloe.

Please know that Chloe's family and friends are working hard to meet your retrial, parole, and prison transfer demands. We do not feel we can ask for the automatic release of anyone, but we hope you will agree to an appeal process in those cases too. This is a long process and there are many obstacles, but we are trying to rush it along. Please be kind to Chloe. She has never harmed a soul in her life. Please tell her we all love her and miss her and we know she will come back to us.

Thank you,

Allegra Mills

CHAPTER 9

He left. I wanted to sleep, but every small noise startled me, even the sound of my own body moving on the mattress. I thought I was in a hospital, then in an ambulance, then on a sofa at home. When I remembered that I was in the warehouse, I was afraid that the brutal man would kill the kinder man and come back. He'd break the combination lock and finish me off. Or else this was just another lie, another part of the game they were playing with me, to drive me crazy. I was so anxious and afraid that when I heard the door opening I nearly jumped out of my skin.

"It's me," he said.

He was carrying a cardboard box containing linen, towels, and underwear. He set the box down and put the combination lock in place. I never thought I'd be happy to see that door locked.

He handed me a stuffed monkey, a white T-shirt, and navy sweatpants. "I couldn't find a bear—I wanted to get back right away," he said.

I put on the improvised pajamas. The T-shirt was twice my size, but the sweatpants were a woman's small.

I found it strangely comforting that the T-shirt was too big for me; it was as if I were being protected by someone larger and stronger. The sweatpants smelled of lavender and I wondered whether they belonged to the woman who had been on the plane with us.

My hostage-taker mopped the floor with strong cleanser

and opened the door to let in fresh air. "If it's okay with you, I would also like to check your temperature," he said.

"Is this your T-shirt?" I asked.

"Yes. I brought you some pills for fever and pain, and something for your stomach."

He handed me two pills and I swallowed them. I hoped they weren't arsenic. *No, he needs me alive*, I thought. *He wouldn't have bought me the monkey.* Then I swallowed a teaspoon of something pink from a bottle. He began shaking a thin glass thermometer.

"What are you doing?"

"Bringing the mercury down."

"Why don't you have a normal thermometer?" I asked, suddenly afraid again.

"I have a digital one, but it doesn't work properly."

I slid the thermometer under my tongue. When the minute was up, I squinted at it but couldn't see anything. "I can't read it," I told him.

He took a look. "Just move it until you get the right light. 103.2. You have to drink more water or you'll dehydrate."

"I want to go home," I wailed.

He sat down next to the bed and said, "I'll stay until you fall asleep."

"I can't sleep," I told him. "When I shut my eyes I see him. I see him in a tunnel."

"Do you want me to read to you?" he asked.

I nodded. He began reading *David Copperfield* from where I'd left off, and I fell asleep to the sound of his voice.

Special Chloe Issue

ALL PEOPLE

Exclusive Interview with Determined Mother Allegra Mills

Photo Album: Inside Chloe's Home

Gymnastics Coach Reveals: Why Chloe Quit

Experts Analyze Chloe's Letter

Chloe's IQ in Genius Range

Interview with Allegra Mills

llegra Mills was teaching a jazz ballet class at her Happy Sprites Dance School in Chicago when the phone call came. The caller was the father of her daughter's best friend, Angie Shaw; Allegra's heart froze at the sound of his voice. Her worst fears were confirmed when Reggie Shaw told her that her daughter, Chloe, had gone missing in Greece. Allegra talks about the roller coaster of pain and hope that followed the devastating news.

Allegra talks about the roller coaster of pain and hope that followed the devastating news.

First let me ask you—how are you?

ALLEGRA: The question has to be, for me, how is Chloe? I don't have time to think about myself.

I think everyone is impressed by your strength and the campaigning you've been doing. Do you feel you're improving Chloe's chances of coming home safely?

ALLEGRA: Yes, I think our work is crucial in every way.

It must be hard to read the darker scenarios that are being imagined.

ALLEGRA: I know people are concerned and concern makes the imagination run riot. My imagination would run riot too, if I let it. But it doesn't help anyone. Nor does it help to blame anyone.

I would not be so forgiving of the organizers of the volunteer program.

ALLEGRA: I can't waste energy on blaming anyone. The main thing is for people not to forget about Chloe.

I don't think there's any chance of that happening. She sounds like a very special person.

ALLEGRA: Yes, she is. I'm truly lucky.

(continued on p. 87)

CHAPTER 10

I woke up covered in sweat. My T-shirt was clinging to me and the sheets felt as if they'd been immersed in water.

It was dark out, but my hostage-taker had left the light on in the bathroom and I saw that he was curled up in a sleeping bag at the other end of the warehouse. I wondered whether I should wake him, but as it turned out, I didn't need to decide. I began to cough, and the sound woke him. He sat up abruptly. He was wearing a white T-shirt, but he quickly pulled on his long-sleeved white shirt and buttoned it.

"I need a shower," I said.

"I'll turn on the boiler," he answered. He disappeared into the bathroom, then returned to the bed with a bottle of water.

"I'm all sweaty," I said.

"I'll change the sheets while you're in the shower."

"How long have I been asleep?"

"Nearly fourteen hours."

When the water had warmed up, I showered, wrapped myself in a clean towel, and came back to bed. It was wonderful being clean again.

He sat on the edge of the mattress and said, "If you tell me what happened, I can try to figure out what might be wrong with you."

I took his hand and held it to my cheek. It was a beautiful hand, and I kissed it. I had no idea why—it wasn't something I'd planned. I was just happy to be feeling better, and I felt grateful—if not to him, then to the higher powers that had saved me. Or maybe I was just going mad with loneliness.

He immediately pulled away. "Please remember that you're here because of me," he said.

"Are you the leader?" I asked.

"No, I'm not any kind of leader."

"But you decide things?"

"Not this. This was completely out of bounds. Nothing like it will happen again. Do you think you can tell me what happened?"

But for some reason, I didn't want to tell him. I didn't want to tell anyone.

"It will help me figure out what's wrong with you," he said.

"Ask your friend," I said, turning my back to him.

"That's not possible."

"Didn't he tell you?"

"Not the details, no."

"What did he say?" I asked.

"Only that he'd been here, and that he'd scared you a little." I felt his anger returning.

"I'm so glad I had that shower. I feel better now. Will you read to me again?"

It was a childish request, but I didn't care. He'd brought me to this; it was his fault I was sick and alone and helpless. When he'd read to me earlier, I'd been able to imagine that he wasn't my captor at all. I wanted to feel that again, even if it was only an illusion.

He began to read, and I fell asleep almost immediately.

I don't remember the next day clearly. I was in an odd

state between sleep and wakefulness and I kept having hallu-cinatory nightmares. In one of them I became convinced that there were slimy, scaly creatures hiding in the warehouse. I crouched on the bed screaming, and my hostage-taker crouched next to me and tried to calm me down. I held on to his arm. "They're in the room, they're in the room," I insisted. "I'll make them go away," he said. "I know a magic spell."

Later I didn't know whether he had really crouched on my bed and talked to me, or whether that too had been part of the dream. It seemed unlikely that he'd say anything about a magic spell.

During the day, he came and went, but at night he slept in the warehouse, in his sleeping bag. He was afraid to leave me alone for too long, in case I got worse. Maybe he also wanted to make sure the other man wouldn't come again, even if he'd changed the lock.

He made me potato soup, which I ate with salted crackers. I swallowed the pills and the pink medicine. Every few hours he handed me the thermometer.

I liked the little stuffed monkey. He had brown fur, worried eyes, a happy, friendly smile, and long, spindly arms. I held him next to me, and even talked to him a little. "Poor you," I told him. "You're stuck here with me now. We'll make the best of it."

My hostage-taker had also brought me a man's watch, which I asked him to set near the bed. The watch anchored me, reminding me that in the outside world time was passing.

Chloe Mills Commodities Doing Brisk Business

Stores everywhere have been selling banners, T-shirts, and other merchandise connected with U.S. hostage Chloe Mills, who is being held captive in an unknown country by terrorists demanding a prisoner exchange. The products convey messages calling for the high school student's release and are among the top best-sellers in their category this month.

Asked whether she was concerned about possible exploitation of her daughter's situation, Chloe's mother, Allegra Mills, said, "I hope and trust that these enterprises have been spurred by concern for Chloe. I'm overwhelmed and moved by the public's support."

Ms. Mills, along with Angie Shaw, the teenager who was in Greece with Chloe at the time she was abducted, have initiated a fundraising campaign to help meet the terrorists' demands, which include costly legal intervention.

Criminal lawyer Jay T. Boyd is heading the team at reduced fees, according to a colleague in the Chicago office of Boyd and Dunlop. "Our work is unrelated to the demands of the terrorists," Boyd emphasized. "We are looking at these cases purely from motives of what is fair and correct and to see whether justice has been served."

A website, www.free-chloe.org, has been receiving daily visits in the tens of thousands.

POST REPORT

CHAPTER II

On the fourth or fifth day I began to feel a little better. My appetite returned and I ate bowl after bowl of vegetable stew and rice. I was learning to read my hostage-taker's body language and his movements, and I could tell as I ate that he was relieved. His face remained expressionless, but his eyes seemed full of hidden messages, and his body was as expressive as an actor's, though I felt sure he wasn't aware of it.

The next evening he brought a stethoscope and asked if I would let him listen to my lungs. A surge of panic tore through me. There was something unspeakably creepy about that stethoscope, and all my distrust returned. *He must be psychotic*, I thought, *imagining he's a doctor.*

"How would you know how to use a stethoscope?" I asked. My stomach was doing somersaults and I knew I looked as frightened as I felt.

He said, "It's not complicated."

"I don't know … It's scary. I mean, if you're a kidnapper and also … like a double personality." It didn't make sense, looking for reassurance from the person I needed to be reassured about, but there was no one else.

He didn't answer. He looked at me steadily, waiting for me to decide.

"I don't know what to think," I cried out, tears coming to my eyes. "The only person I can ask is you, but how can I believe anything you say?"

"Yes, it's a hard situation for you."

"Why do you need to listen to my lungs?"

"I'm worried because your fever is not going down. Maybe you've contracted pneumonia."

"How would you know if I had pneumonia?"

"If you had fluid in your lungs I might hear a crackling sound. You could try to hear yourself, if you like. You know, it would help me very much if you told me what happened."

"Why don't you ask your friend?" I said angrily.

"I can't explain that to you," he replied.

"I can't believe you don't know."

"I don't know. That's why I'm asking you. The pail was overturned, the floor was covered with water. That's all I know. I can imagine some things, but I don't know."

"I may have swallowed some dirty water," I relented. I felt degraded, talking about what happened—as degraded as I'd felt when it happened.

"From the floor?" he asked, his rage returning.

"The floor? No, in the pail …"

"He dunked you?"

"Yes."

He folded his arms and his body was tense with disgust. But his voice was unaffected. He asked, "Anything else?"

"No."

"Well, do I get to listen to your lungs?"

"All right."

He sat behind me and I felt the cold stethoscope on my back. "What if you're some sort of schizophrenic pretending to be a doctor?" I asked. "Isn't there a movie like that?"

"There are probably many movies like that."

"Horror movies," I said. "What do you hear?"

"I can't hear anything if you talk. If you just inhale deeply, that will help me."

I breathed for him, and he listened to different parts of my back for a long time. He seemed to know what he was doing after all, and I began to relax. I couldn't be so unintuitive that I wouldn't know an ordinary person from a psychopath.

"Your lungs sound okay," he said. "Have you any pain anywhere?"

"No."

"Can I just check a few things?"

"Yes," I said. It felt strange, letting him examine me—it was as if we were in a play or some kind of bizarre reality show. But I didn't have any choice. I wanted to get better.

He touched the glands along my throat and pounded my lower back to check my kidneys; then I lay down and he lightly pressed parts of my stomach. He had unusual hands, an unusual touch. Gentle, alive, communicative. Like his eyes, his fingers compensated for his expressionless face and unemotional voice.

Or maybe it only seemed that way because I was so isolated, and being touched made me feel less alone. It was confusing, seeing this side of him, and my confusion tired me out.

"I don't usually get sick," I told him.

"Did the man come near you?" he asked, moving away and also looking away.

I knew what he meant and I said quickly, "Oh God, no. No."

I shuddered. Bad as it was, it could have been worse. *Well, everything can be worse,* I thought. *So what?*

"You're angry at him?" I asked because I needed to hear him say it again.

"Yes, of course. More than angry."

"Because he almost killed me? Because he did it behind your back? If it *was* behind your back," I added, more to myself than to him.

"I'll make you tea," he said. He rose from the bed and placed the kettle on the hot plate.

I had an irrational sense of being abandoned and, trying to draw him back in, I continued desperately, "That's what happens when you become a criminal." I began to shiver with cold. I sat up and draped the army blanket over my shoulders. "You end up hanging out with people like that. What if he kills you? And then I won't have you to protect me."

"That's something you don't have to worry about."

He handed me a mug of tea and I held it against my chest. "Why am I shivering?" I asked.

"Your body is seeking to balance out its temperature."

"Who are you?" I asked, pleading with him for an answer, though I knew he couldn't provide one.

I began to feel sick again. "I don't feel well," I said, throwing off the blanket. "Now I'm hot. Could you open the door again, please?"

He undid the combination lock and opened the door. Sweet-smelling air filled the warehouse and made me sleepy. I wanted to shut my eyes, but though my nightmares had subsided, I was still haunted by the image of the tunnel whenever I shut my eyes. "Will you read to me?" I whispered. I didn't know if he could hear me; I could barely hear myself.

"If you like."

"Why are you kind to me?"

"The goal is for my friend to be released, not to make you suffer."

"What if they make one of those police drawings of you?"

"No one will suspect me."

"Such a nice smell coming from outside. Can I step out, just for a few minutes?"

"When you're better," he said.

"Really?"

"Yes."

I didn't believe him. I lay down and he resumed reading from where we'd left off. David Copperfield had been sent to school by his evil stepfather and Steerforth had taken his money. At first you're sure Steerforth is tricking David, but he uses the money to buy food for everyone so David will be popular with the other boys. Steerforth benefits from the party, but so does David.

I could tell my hostage-taker was enjoying the story as well. It was pleasant listening to him; he had a nice reading voice. I realized that I'd stopped noticing his foreign accent. I interrupted him to ask, "Do you know the story?"

"I never read it until now."

I felt a sudden rush of affection for him. "You're cute," I said. I wasn't usually spontaneous like that, just blurting out a passing thought without considering whether I really meant it or how it might sound.

But it was as if nothing mattered anymore. I could say anything, do anything, because none of this was real. It was something else altogether. Not a game or a movie but something disconnected from reality.

"Let's focus on getting you through this," he said.

"I think music might help me sleep."

"I'll try to come up with something. Is there anything in particular you'd like? I can't remember what it said in the newspaper."

"The newspaper?"

"Yes, there is much information about you in the media. We got lucky with you. Your story sells many copies."

"You're just making that up," I accused him.

He went over to his briefcase, pulled out a newspaper, tore out a large photo, and held it up for me to see. It was the photo he'd taken of me, with the black cloth in the background. I looked sad and afraid.

I reached out for it, but he wouldn't let me have it—he didn't want me to see the other side of the page.

It was a little strange, being in the news, but I was glad I hadn't been forgotten.

"I need to write my mom another letter," I insisted. I felt a wild desire to communicate with her.

"I can read what it says here. She's quoted."

I felt like screaming in frustration. Why hadn't he volunteered that information? "Tell me, tell me," I urged impatiently.

He read: "'I can't talk about the case because it would interfere with the work of the police, but I feel confident that my daughter is safe and that no harm will come to her. She is a sweet, lovely person, and I can't imagine anyone wanting to hurt her. If she sees this, I want her to know that everyone is thinking about her and everything is under control. I love you, sweetheart.'"

"Read it again," I said. It was deeply, wonderfully consoling, hearing those words. A connection to the outside world, a connection to my mom, reassurance that she hadn't fallen apart. I couldn't understand why he hadn't told me about the message right away. Didn't he know how desperately I needed to hear it?

I made him read the quote a third time, so I could write down the exact words in my notebook, though I already knew them by heart. I was crying with relief and homesickness.

"Why didn't you let me know sooner?" I asked. I shut my eyes and drifted off into an uneasy sleep. In my dreams Mom stood waving to me behind a glass door, but when I touched the door it turned into a sheet of flames.

Prosecutor Mayfair-Horrick Dies from Post-Operative Complications

Public prosecutor Lawrence Mayfair-Horrick died in Durham, North Carolina, this morning from complications following heart surgery.

Mayfair-Horrick, an outspoken figure known for his controversial comments and ruthless courtroom style, has come to worldwide attention in the wake of the abduction of Chicago teenager Chloe Mills in Greece two months ago.

The demands of the terrorists focus on prisoners they term "victims" of Mayfair-Horrick.

Mayfair-Horrick did not comment on the abduction before he died, apart from saying that he took no interest in accusations made against him.

"We were aware of many of these cases," said Martin Soames, executive director of the Indigent Defense Services of Durham. "I abhor terrorist tactics. I am in favor of a review of possible irregularities in which Mayfair-Horrick was involved, but there is no connection between my support for such a review and the abduction of Chloe Mills."

POST REPORT

CHAPTER 12

The next day my fever had shot up. "Maybe I need antibiotics," I said.

"I don't think so. This seems to be viral. But a very stubborn virus."

"My stomach is better."

"Yes, but your fever isn't subsiding. I think we should try sponging you down. If it's all right with you."

He changed the sheets and I lay on the bed in my underwear, a bath towel draped over me. He ran a wet washcloth along my legs and arms and shoulders and face. It was such a relief to feel my body cooling down that I asked him to do it several times during the next few hours. By evening my fever was down to 99.

"It seems to have worked," he said. "I think you're finally starting to recover."

"Thank you."

He didn't answer. He didn't like being thanked.

Because I was feeling better, my mood improved. "What day is it?" I asked him as he set the table for the evening meal. I noticed that he was only setting for one.

"The less you know, the better."

I'd never met anyone like him—it was strange, the way he hardly ever betrayed emotion when he spoke, the way he kept his face still and impassive. It was as if he was absent, almost. But his penetrating eyes, and what he actually said, the way he listened to me and seemed to understand me, those things showed that he was very far from absent.

He sat beside me on the bed and took my wrist in order to check my pulse. He rested my arm on his knee and looked at his watch, counting the beats.

When he was through, he didn't let go right away. His gaze lingered on my arm, and it seemed to me that his eyes softened. Then he snatched his hand away and stood up abruptly, as if embarrassed.

I was aware of a tingling sensation creeping through me, starting at the spot on my wrist where his two fingers had rested and spreading to the rest of my body. What was that all about?

He said, "I think since you're feeling much better, I'll leave you now. I'm sorry not to stay to eat with you. I have much to do that has fallen behind."

I saw that he really was looking tired. Well, I wasn't going to feel sorry for him! It served him right.

"Imagine if people who know you knew what you were doing after hours. I'll bet they'd be surprised."

"I'll try to come the day after tomorrow. If your fever goes up again, go back to taking the pills, two every four hours. I'm leaving the bottle here on the table."

"Whatever."

"You've been very great," he told me.

I felt beyond annoyed when he said that. Complimenting me for being cooperative seemed somewhat ironic, under the circumstances. What else could I have done, other than try to appease him? He was keeping me alive.

I replied bitterly, "How—by lying here in bed?"

He pretended not to notice my anger. "You can write another letter to your mother while I'm gone," he said. "Please keep it to half a page."

"How is she?"

"She's strong like you."

"You have a lot of nerve," I said. "Making our lives hell, then congratulating us on not falling apart."

His response was a silent gaze. I looked into his intelligent eyes, eyes that seemed to say so much more than he was willing to tell me, and my anger evaporated. My emotions kept changing, and it confused me. I wasn't used to not knowing how I felt. Angie was the emotional one; she was the one who leaped from one mood to another in a matter of seconds. The smallest things upset her—a rude cashier or a broken zipper—but even smaller things cheered her up: a bowl of grapes, a cloud in the shape of a shoe.

"How's Angie?" I asked.

"I can see she's very devoted to you. You're lucky to have such a good friend."

"If I ever see her again …" I said, pouting, though I was no longer worried about being killed. I'd pushed that thought away, and it stayed away.

"I'll try to bring more of the things you asked for," he said.

"Especially music."

He looked at me, and his eyes were full of complicated messages, but I couldn't untangle them.

He packed his things and undid the combination lock. Without warning, I began to sob. My sobs took me by surprise. I wasn't crying, my nose wasn't running, but I couldn't stop sobbing. He stepped outside and locked the door behind him. I continued sobbing for a long time.

Chloe Come Home

Every Wednesday is Chloe Day
Please Join Us as We
Demonstrate for Actions
That Will Facilitate
Chloe's Release
Meeting Place:
Your Town Hall, 7 pm

For more information,
please visit www.free-chloe.org

CHAPTER 13

Later that evening I wrote another letter to Mom. I thought of inserting a secret code that spelled out *warehouse near forest and aluminum fence in industrial compound, arrived by private plane with man and woman.*

But I couldn't think of any code my hostage-taker wouldn't be able to see through.

In the end the letter was almost identical to the first one, because there was so much I wasn't allowed to say.

I felt very depressed when I'd finished writing.

I thought about all the fights I'd had with Mom. It was always the same fight, about the same thing. Mom used our big old house, which my father inherited from a great-aunt, as a hostel for freeloaders from her past. She traveled a lot when she was younger, and she met all sorts of bohemian types from the world of dance and theater. She kept in touch with them, and as soon as she heard that anyone was having a hard time, she invited the person to stay with us.

She didn't consult me, and I found myself sharing my home with an endless stream of people I didn't know and often didn't like.

I kept telling Mom we couldn't afford to support these people. Once my father died, our entire income came from the dance school. Mom worked long hours, seven days a week; there were always crises and problems to be solved. While she solved them, I was left alone in the house with her guests. Some of them were all right, but most were eccentric and often messy, though Mom did set some ground rules—no smoking, no drinking. I added a rule of my own: no one allowed in my room.

When I was little, the guests babysat me, so their presence at least made some sense. But when I got old enough to be left on my own, I didn't want them around, and I complained and sulked. I was rude to the visitors I didn't like, I accused Mom of imposing weirdos on me. "It's like living in a hotel with random strangers!" I used to exclaim, sometimes within earshot of the guests. Then I'd storm out and sleep over at Angie's.

I felt wretched, thinking about those outbursts. How could I have been so selfish and childish? I was telling Mom off for being a kind-hearted, generous person. Now that I myself was so alone, I understood that she'd done it partly to help her friends, but also because she was lonely. She wasn't interested in dating after my dad died, and she was too busy with the dance school and with bringing me up to make new friends.

Maybe I resented that I wasn't enough for her, that she wanted adult company and more variety. Maybe I was jealous. Instead of enjoying the presence of interesting people and making them feel at home, instead of being glad that Mom had so many friends, I acted like an obnoxious brat.

Guilt and regret fueled my depression. Mom must have been disappointed with her selfish, control-freak daughter. When I bitched about the wet towels in the bathroom and the empty mugs in the living room it was my own obsessive personality that was the problem. And now I might never have a chance to tell her how sorry I was.

If only Dad hadn't died! I was six when he died, and for a

long time I didn't accept that he was never coming back. For several years, whenever I was at a gymnastics meet or in Mom's end-of-year dance show, I imagined that Dad was in the audience. My grandparents came over almost every day at first, and Dad began to get blurred with my granddad, who looked and spoke a lot like him.

Now, suddenly, I felt myself plunging into a bottomless well of grief. It was as if I was experiencing Dad's death for the first time.

I began to wail inconsolably. *Daddy, Daddy*, I cried over and over. I didn't know how I'd be able to cope with so much anguish.

Memories of my father came back to me—climbing on his shoulders when he read the paper, playing Hungry Bear at dinner, painting the garage with him. He'd made a big heart for me on the wall; I wanted it to stay forever, and I cried when he painted over it. He laughed and took me out for ice cream.

I thought about the storybooks and poems he read to me at bedtime. He loved poetry and even though I was small he read me poems written for adults—

On either side the river lie, long fields of barley and of rye ...

I loved that poem, though I thought the Lady of Shalott was the lady of shallot, named after the fields of barley and rye and shallots. I wished I had that poem now.

She hath no loyal knight and true, the Lady of Shalott.

I cried myself to sleep. It was a long, deep sleep and when I woke I felt heavy and groggy. My depression was like a physical weight pressing down on me. I didn't want to move, but eventually I got up to eat. Then I returned to bed and lay there for a long time. Cockroaches attacked the dirty dishes I left on the table. I watched them with apathy. I didn't care about anything, and I couldn't imagine ever feeling better. The world was a bleak, horrible place, full of cruelty and misery. How could anyone be happy in it?

I was alone for two and a half days. I only got up to eat and go to the bathroom. I didn't bother showering or brushing my hair and I slept most of the time. My hostage-taker had brought me many of the things I'd asked for—skin lotion, slippers, a hairbrush—but they only made me feel worse. They were a confirmation that this was now my life, this was where I lived.

My hostage-taker returned at noon on the third day. He didn't say anything about the mess. He was loaded down with groceries, and he began tidying up.

I turned my back to him and lay in bed facing the wall.

He said, "Do you have the letter for your mother?" I couldn't tell if he was just making conversation or if he wanted to get the transaction over with.

"It's inside *David Copperfield*," I mumbled, still not looking at him.

"I brought you some music. Do you want to listen to something?"

"I don't care."

I heard a few clicks, and then the exotic sounds of an old

Sting favorite—"Desert Rose"—ringing out in the silence, but it didn't penetrate my dark mood.

"I also brought you *Beginners' Italian* and a few more books."

I didn't bother replying—what was there to say?

"Do you want me to go?" he asked.

"I don't care."

"Maybe I'll stay just for dinner. I brought some chilled white wine, if your stomach is up to it. And I turned on the boiler, in case you want to shower."

I wondered vaguely if I smelled. I hadn't done more than splash water on my face in two and a half days.

When the shower was ready, I found a present waiting for me there: a basket filled with tiny bottles of fruit-scented shampoos, conditioners, body washes, a variety of delicious-smelling carved soaps.

What does it say about me that strawberry shampoo and pine-scented soap made me so happy? I felt my depression lifting, and by the time I'd finished washing my hair I was in a good mood.

I realized that I'd almost forgotten, since my abduction, what it was like, a good mood—though that had been the usual thing for me. The sadness I'd felt about my father was still there, but it had moved to its own corner, covered itself with a blanket, and gone to sleep for now.

I dressed, rubbed my hair with a towel, and went straight to the CDs he'd brought me. The one with "Desert Rose" had ended and I was desperate for more music.

I looked through the pile but there were no labels, so I chose a disk at random and slid it in the player. Another song I liked, "First Day of My Life," came on. Was my taste in music really in the news? It seemed farfetched.

I looked up at my hostage-taker. He was sitting at the table, reading one of the stories in the anthology he'd brought me.

All at once I remembered a dream I'd had about him. I must have remembered it in the morning, but I'd gone back to sleep and forgotten all about it.

In the dream my hostage-taker was swimming toward me. At first he was swimming in water and then in fields of barley and rye. I was surprised that it was possible to swim through fields but then I realized that plants gave you more support than water and also that you couldn't drown, and I thought, *What a good idea—why doesn't everyone swim in fields?* The movements of his arms were strong and gentle and in the dream he was compassionate and good. I realized that I'd been wrong about him. He was there to save me, not to hurt me. I wanted to join him, and in the dream I felt I loved him.

Now, partly under the spell of the dream and partly under the spell of the fragrant soaps, I felt an overpowering urge to throw my arms around him. He seemed sweet to me, sitting there at the table, waiting to eat with me.

He was kind, too. He'd saved my life, and it wasn't his fault that things had gone wrong with the other man. That sort of thing happened all the time, at least in movies.

I liked his hands, his sensuous mouth, his eyes. I liked his expressive body and the way he listened to me. He had brought me a stuffed monkey when I was sick, and now he'd brought me a gift basket he knew I'd like. It meant he felt bad for me, it meant he was really trying.

And apart from everything else, I was just happy to see him. I was happy he'd come back. I walked over to where he was sitting and, standing behind him, I clasped my arms around his neck.

Everything about him suggested that he was unapproachable. He was too serious, too restrained. He seemed untouchable. Some people are like that—they give you the message that they don't want you to come close, they don't want you to touch them. He'd set up a barrier around himself, and it wasn't negotiable.

But he'd broken all the rules by abducting me. He'd broken the law and he'd changed the rules of ordinary life. That meant I could change the rules too. It meant there weren't any rules—not here, not now.

And so I casually laid my arms on his shoulders and crossed them. It was bliss, feeling his shoulder muscles under my arms, feeling his body close to mine. My cheek brushed his hair, and my own hair fell on his neck.

I knew he'd move away. He carefully lifted my arms and without turning said, very firmly, "No." I was a little afraid of that tone of voice. It was the first time he'd sounded slightly less casual, slightly less composed.

I sat down opposite him. It was wonderful having music—"The Scientist" was on now. The song seemed to be about us. *Yes, tell me all your secrets*, I wanted to say.

He put the bottle of wine away, as if afraid of what I might do if I drank. I fought back my fear—he hadn't meant to hurt my feelings. He was just making a point. "Can't I hug you?" I asked.

"No," he said, back to his usual self. He began slicing a loaf of olive bread.

"Why? Why can't I hug you?"

"You know why."

"No, I don't."

"Let's eat, we can talk about it later. Would you like some bread?"

"'Would you like some bread?'" I echoed, imitating his serious, formal voice. "Yes, that would be lovely, thank you," I answered in a fake British accent.

"I'm glad you're in a better mood."

"Any more messages from my mom? Tell me everything about her. And my grandparents, and Angie. Why can't you bring me a newspaper? Or print something off the Net?"

"Everyone is fine, the message is exactly the same as last time. There's nothing in the papers that you don't know."

"I'd still like to see it. I'm going crazy, being so cut off."

"I'll see what I can do," he said, but I could tell he wasn't planning to do anything. He didn't want me to see magazines or newspapers, and he didn't want to say why.

"I was really down yesterday and the day before," I told him. "And this morning."

"Yes, I noticed. It's from being alone and because of what happened to you."

"Oh, really?" I said sarcastically. "Who would have thought."

"I'm sorry I couldn't come. I won't always be able to come, I'll have to miss some days."

I said, a little frantically, "You promised to let me out. Even if just for five minutes. I promise I won't run away. You can tie a rope around my waist."

He tilted his head. "In fact, I was going to suggest sitting outside for a few minutes. You're looking pale. But I don't think we'll have to resort to the methods of Silas Marner."

"I know that story! We did it in school ... You're smart. You know a lot. Did you go to school in England?"

"No."

"But you have a British accent. On top of your other accent."

He didn't answer.

"Can we go out now?"

"Why don't we eat first?"

"All right," I agreed. "Something to look forward to." I lifted the loaf of olive bread to my face and inhaled. It had a wonderful homemade smell. "I'll gain weight here," I said. "What does it say about me in the paper?"

"Nothing new."

"That's so weird," I said. "I guess I'm famous now."

"I'd say so."

"Well, at least I haven't been forgotten."

"Far from it."

"Thanks for the bath stuff, by the way."

"I'll bring you a tennis set next time."

"Great. What are people saying about me?"

"There are a lot of guesses about what's happening to you, whether you're alive, what sort of people are holding you. That's all."

"What are they guessing?"

"The worst, of course," he said, sipping the white wine.

"Like what?" I asked.

"Like all the things you were worried about when you first arrived."

"Creepy," I said. Suddenly the idea of people inventing horror stories about me was repellent—even scary, for some reason.

"You can be forgotten as soon as you get back, if you want."

I watched him as he ate. He cut everything before eating it, even bread, and the pieces were always tiny. Or if the food couldn't be cut, he put tiny bits on his fork. He seemed barely to chew. "What do you have against being hugged?" I asked him.

"I don't want to benefit from you in any way," he said. His answer surprised me. He was admitting that he would enjoy it if I hugged him. *He likes me*, I thought.

"But I'm the one who needs you."

He didn't answer immediately. He stared at me, but I was used to his stares and I stared back. Finally he said, "I don't want your forgiveness. I've taken away your freedom, and I almost let you die. If we manage to maintain some kind of equilibrium, we're doing well. Anything else would be completely inappropriate."

"Fine!" I said, slouching in my chair. Trying to cover my embarrassment, I grumbled, "You know, you're a very poor hostage-taker. You're not supposed to care so much about me. Didn't you read the hostage-taking manual?"

He tilted his head sideways again, as if trying to see me from a different angle; I knew by now that this was his way of smiling. He said, "I understand your desire to joke, but it's a serious matter after all. Women are almost always exploited in these situations. You narrowly escaped such a disaster yourself."

"You think I want to be harmed? I'm not a masochist."

"I think it's hard for you to see clearly right now."

"You're so patronizing!" I said, sinking my teeth into a deep-fried croquette of some sort. Eating was a welcome distraction from being rejected. I was starving, and I helped myself to seconds of everything.

"I'm glad to see your appetite has returned," he said.

"What else did you read about me? Apart from that I used to do gymnastics?"

"I don't follow everything, there's too much."

"Too much?"

"You're a good story for the media. Attractive, talented seventeen-year-old in captivity, someone people can watch on YouTube."

"That's not my fault, the school posted it. They post all their competitions."

"I was quite impressed."

"I don't know how I feel about all that publicity."

"The coverage is all very positive," he assured me.

"There's not much to say, I've had a pretty boring life so far."

"The media can always find something, if they try hard enough."

Neither of us spoke for a few minutes. I put another CD in the player—this one was classical, and the enchanted melody of "Moonlight Sonata" floated in the air.

My hostage-taker produced a paper bag filled with chocolate-chip cookies. I fished one out and munched on it. It was the best chocolate-chip cookie I'd ever had. "You're a very good cook," I said. "Maybe you should consider a career in the catering business instead of hostage-taking."

"I can't stay long today, but I'll be back tomorrow."

"Do you have a job?"

"I'll just do the washing up and then we can go out for a few minutes."

He carried the dishes to the old rusty sink in the bathroom and began washing them. I sat down on the toilet lid and watched him. I was in a mischievous mood. I felt like a little kid who wants to pester the babysitter. "You missed a spot," I said.

"You really are feeling better."

"This place is crawling with roaches."

"Yes, there's not much to be done about that. Once you have them, they're hard to get rid of."

I yawned. "I think I felt one on my foot during the night.

Yuck!"

"I think they avoid people," he said.

"Oh no, no, no, you're wrong! Very wrong. You aren't up on your cockroach information at all. My granddad lived in Cyprus when he was young, and he said the cockroaches traveled all over his face at night."

"That must have been quite an infestation."

I stood up, yawned again, and leaned slightly against his arm. Not in any serious way—more the way you'd lean on someone at a party, just for fun. He was much taller than me—I only reached the top of his shoulder blades.

He put down the dish he was washing, dried his hands, and moved away from me.

He carried the washed dishes to the table and stacked them on a towel. Then he turned to me. "Once and for all, this has to end."

"You're so serious about everything. Can't you relax a little?"

"This isn't an easy situation for you or for me. It would be strange if I felt relaxed about it."

"Whatever," I sulked.

"You aren't yourself. People want to feel safe and in control, so they identify with the aggressor in their lives—I'm sure you can see that. You're acting out of loneliness and denial."

"Denial? Denial about what? You think I can actually forget that I'm cooped up in here all day like a caged animal!"

"Denial about my role in your life. It's true that I'm doing what I can to make things easier for you, but I'm the one who's locked you up here in the first place."

"You're so patronizing," I repeated.

"I'm only trying to explain."

"It's the appearance of exploitation that worries you?" I asked.

"Not the appearance, the reality."

"It would look like you were taking advantage of me?"

"It would look that way and it would be that way," he said.

It was the second time he was admitting that he was attracted to me. He just didn't think it was right to act on those feelings.

"Not if I'm the one deciding," I pointed out.

He said, "There must be equality in a partnership. We aren't equals now. You're angry with me, but anger is hard to sustain, so you transform it into something else. Think about it logically. You don't know anything about me, only that I've taken away your freedom."

"Okay, okay. I get the point."

"You have to force yourself to be logical."

"You sound like Spock. Do you know *Star Trek*?"

"Yes."

I stared at him. I was partly embarrassed by the whole situation, partly glad that we were really talking. I said, "Logically, I feel what I feel. And what I feel is that I love you."

I had no idea I was going to say those words, and they shocked me as much as they shocked him. I could tell he was upset, though he tried not show it.

I turned away from him in confusion. I didn't know why I'd spoken out that way, or whether I regretted it. But I did know that the words I'd said were true. I loved him.

He stood up. "If you continue on this track I won't stay here. I'll bring you the things you need and go."

"Fine!" I snapped again. I was hurt, and also angry. He was taking even the little control I had away from me. "You make all the decisions here, excuse me for forgetting that! Do whatever you want. I don't care if you stay or not. I don't care if I never see you again!"

"Do you want to go out for some fresh air before I leave?"

"Yes," I said crossly. "Yes, of course I want to go outside. Sorry I have to bother you with my presence."

He scrounged around in one of the bags and handed me a large white shawl, oversized sunglasses, and a black hat with a floppy rim—probably the one they'd made me wear when I was abducted. "Pull the hat down low, please," he instructed, "and wrap yourself in the shawl. And you must promise not to give me a hard time."

"So I'm not allowed to shout *help* at the top of my lungs?"

"I'm glad you haven't lost your sense of humor."

We stepped out of the warehouse, taking the two chairs with us. There was a narrow navy blue awning along the front wall of the warehouse; I hadn't noticed it before. But even under the awning, with the sunglasses on and the hat shading my face, the sunlight hurt my eyes, and I had to keep them shut for a few seconds.

Then I looked up at the blue sky. I was stunned by the

sky, the stones on the ground, the dry grass and purple weeds growing along the edges of the warehouse. It was as though I'd only ever seen those things in photographs.

"I've already forgotten what grass looks like," I said. "And I've only been in this stupid warehouse for two weeks."

"Yes, it happens fast. I'm not often able to be here during the day, but when I am we'll try to sit outside."

We set the chairs against the wall and sat down. I lifted my head to the sun. I was so grateful to be outdoors that my anger dissolved. I plucked a weed, twirled it in my hand, brought it to my face. "One thing about being confined," I said. "It makes you appreciate things. I never thought a weed could be so amazing. My mom says 'Chloe' means the shoot of a plant in Greek. Hello, Chloe …" I said giddily.

I looked around me. The view was blocked on both sides—by the aluminum fence on my right, and the cement wall of a building on my left. But the forest up ahead was magnificent. My eyes absorbed every twisting tree branch, every shade of green. I'd never noticed the millions of details in the world around me. Angie did, because she had an artist's eye, but I'd always taken my surroundings for granted.

"What will I see if I look around the corner?" I asked.

"Only another fence."

"So this is really like a courtyard?"

"Yes, it's closed off."

"Poor Mom. She must be so worried. And Angie—she's anxious even when things are normal."

"They're both working hard for a retrial."

"A retrial? You mean instead of an exchange?"

"A legal process allows them to release someone innocent without seeming to give in to us."

"Sometimes you say 'us' and sometimes you say 'I.' Are you part of a group?"

"The less you know about me, the better."

"Are you the only one I'll see?"

"Yes."

"But … I mean, just the fact that a criminal is asking for this guy's release, wouldn't that be enough to make the prisoner seem guilty? I mean, if that's who his friends are, it's worse for him, not better."

"We made ourselves sound convincingly insane."

I laughed. "So it would seem you chose someone at random?"

"That's right."

"If you sound insane, doesn't that scare my mother?"

"Luckily, she's an optimist."

I linked my fingers and stretched my arms in front of me. "Where's your car?"

"Parked in back."

"Is it also a limo?"

"No, just an ordinary car."

"But that was a private plane … you must be very rich."

He didn't say anything, of course, and we sat in silence for a while. It was so peaceful, sitting there quietly in the sun. No one seeing us would have believed that I was a prisoner and the man sitting next to me was my jailer.

"Time to go back," he said. "I have a lot to do."

"I'd like to see your to-do list. Laundry, shopping, visit hostage …"

It was hard, going back in. I longed to do a cartwheel on the grass. Instead, I had to return to the dreary warehouse.

Without warning, my depression returned. I curled up on the bed and covered myself with the sheet. I began to think about Dad again. I wanted to sleep and sleep, and wake up when it was all over.

Terrorists Holding Chloe "Children of Lord Ruthven"

Homeland Security has revealed that the group holding U.S. teenager Chloe Mills hostage calls itself "Children of Lord Ruthven." Lord Ruthven is the name of a fictional vampire in a 19th-century novel. However, authorities have withheld other details of the group's communications or the means by which information is being transmitted.

The response to the information has included the inauguration of the slogan "CLR—Let Her Go" among supporters of the Free Chloe Campaign. Demonstrators across the globe have been gathering every Wednesday evening to pressure the government to act quickly for Chloe's release.

The Internet has been rife with speculations about the political implications of the name. Some experts are expressing concern over the absence of a clear political affiliation, which could suggest delusional psychosis on the part of the terrorists or a cult-like group, while others see the group's name as a diversionary ploy.

POST REPORT

CHAPTER 14

Over the next few days I struggled against my depression. My occasional dose of sunshine helped, and I was glad to have music in my life again. My hostage-taker brought me a tennis set, which kept me occupied for far longer than I would have imagined.

I also had more books now, including two gorgeous coffee table books—one about Greece and one about the history of Olympic gymnastics.

I wrote out a schedule for myself and tried to follow it:

9:00–9:30	shower, etc.
9:30–10:00	breakfast, dishes
10:00–11:30	wash floor, write in journal, read
11:30–1:00	exercise, tennis
1:00–1:30	lunch, dishes
1:30–3:00	study Italian, do crosswords, read
?	visit from hostage-taker

Days without a visit were the hardest. I'd get cabin fever and I'd feel like tearing my hair out. Attacks of homesickness and loneliness would sweep over me in huge waves. I missed Mom, my friends, my house, my room. I missed Pumpkin and everything else about my life at home, even vacuuming the carpets.

Then, suddenly, my hostage-taker vanished.

I think it was some time between the fourth and fifth week, but I can't be sure because my calendar was pretty hopeless by then. I didn't always remember whether I'd already checked off the day or not, and I also lost track when I was sick. After a while it didn't seem to matter all that much.

He vanished without warning. He said he'd come the next day, but he didn't. He didn't come back the day after that, or the next, or the next. I ran out of food on the fourth day, but my hostage-taker had brought me a box of canned food for emergencies. The labels had been torn off the tins, but there were stickers to identify them: corn, peaches, soup.

The cans kept me going for a day or two. Then the can-opener broke. It split into two and there was no way to fix it. I tried stomping on the cans, hitting them against the wall, pounding them on the edge of the sink, but they only bent out of shape. Then I lost interest and stopped trying. I wasn't hungry anyhow.

I was afraid.

Not just afraid that my hostage-taker had died and that I would starve to death, but also irrationally afraid, the way you are when you're little. I was literally afraid of vampires and monsters and alien creatures—afraid they'd suddenly appear in the warehouse. Every scary movie I'd ever seen came back to me with a vengeance. I kept expecting to see the slasher guy from *Nightmare on Elm Street* sitting on a chair in the corner of the room, grinning at me.

I was afraid to sleep because I was afraid of my dreams, I was afraid to be awake because I was afraid of the things around me. I knew I was losing my mind, and that my terror was the first symptom.

I tried to read, write, exercise, but nothing succeeded in calming me or distracting me from my fear. I clutched my monkey. I held him close to me and wouldn't let him go. He was my only chance, I felt—my only hope for sanity. His sad eyes and friendly smile made me feel I wasn't really alone. I wondered if feeling so attached to a toy monkey was in itself a sign that I was going mad.

I draped the towels across the table so they hung over the sides, and I sat under the table with my monkey, wrapped in my blanket and protected by the towel tent.

Everything terrified me. I tried to sing, but my voice frightened me. I couldn't play any music because it all sounded spooky and malicious, like the soundtrack to a horror movie. I tried to read, but the words made no sense and I began to imagine that they were written in code.

I thought about my life, how short it had been, how sad Mom would be when she found out I was dead. Another part of me wanted to die, because I didn't feel I could bear to live this way much longer.

I took out my lipstick and drew two streaks on either side of my face like a Native American. I remembered that red was the color of war; I hoped it would ward off demons. I was desperate enough to try anything.

I was afraid of suffering. I knew starvation was painful. Even if I somehow managed to open the cans, they'd only last another week, and then I'd have nothing.

I cried and hugged my monkey under the table. "You're my friend," I told him. "My best friend." I kissed his soft fur and held him tighter.

I lost all sense of time. I drifted in and out of nightmarish semi-sleep and I had no idea whether an hour had passed or a day. A few times my nightmares turned into a wonderful dream and I was convinced I was at home, in my bed, and everyone I loved was downstairs with balloons and a cake, waiting for me to come down and celebrate my return. I felt Pumpkin's paws on my chest and his tongue tickling my ears. I'd wake up shivering and sobbing.

I was sitting under the tented table, dressed only in underwear but draped in my blanket, when I heard the door opening. I was too dazed to feel either fear or relief. Through the narrow space between two towels I saw my hostage-taker striding into the warehouse. He walked toward me, crouched down, and peered in. "I couldn't come. I'm sorry."

He'd left the door open because he had a lot of things to unload. I froze for a second, barely believing my luck, and then, with all my remaining strength dashed out and began to run.

It was late evening, but there was still enough light to see the forest ahead. I couldn't run fast because I was barefoot and weak and still clutching the blanket around me.

My hostage-taker came after me, lifted me off the ground, held me over his shoulder. I pounded his back with my fists, though I was dizzy and the ground seemed to be spinning.

He carried me back inside and shut the door. "As soon as you calm down we'll go out for a walk," he said. He handed me a glass of chocolate milk. Nothing had ever tasted so good.

Drinking the milk re-energized me and also renewed my anger. I sprang toward him and began hitting him on his chest and arms. I called him every name I could think of. "I hate you, I hate you!" I shouted. I wanted to kick him, but I wasn't wearing shoes. Instead I bit his arm, hard. I was sure I'd hurt him and I was glad.

"You'll feel better after a walk," he said, trying to move away from me. "We can go to the forest."

"So you can kill me when there's no one around?" I stomped to the bed, held my monkey against my chest, and draped the blanket over my head so I was entirely hidden. I heard him moving around, cleaning up, putting stuff away.

"I'm just going to bring more things from the car," he said. I heard the door opening and shutting.

I peeked out from under the blanket and saw a plate with a snack in the shape of a face: diamond cracker eyes with olive pupils, a brie nose, a comical raisin mouth turned up at one end and down at the other.

The face only made me angrier, and I pushed the plate away.

But I couldn't resist for long. I started nibbling on the snack, and I felt my anger slowly dissolving. I'd never been good at maintaining anger. Much as I wanted to stay angry, much as I was determined to be angry until doomsday, I always gave in. Anger just wasn't any fun; it was too draining. I had no idea how anyone could sustain it for extended periods, though I knew that some people did. I couldn't imagine what it would be like to live that way.

My hostage-taker returned with the last of the groceries. "We can go now," he said, handing me the black hat.

I pulled on my jeans and we stepped outside. I felt dazed and disoriented. It was late evening, but the sun had not yet set, and the sky was palest blue with streaks of gold. I noticed that my hostage-taker was carrying a flashlight—did that mean we'd be staying out until dark?

It was bliss being outdoors. I walked next to my hostage-taker, my monkey still in my arms. We reached the forest and I leaned against one of the trees, pressed my head against the bark, and took a deep breath. My body seemed to be feeding on the sweet night air and I felt the tension seeping out of my limbs. It was over—I was alive after all. And I was no longer afraid of indefinable things. Or at least not as afraid as before. My hostage-taker's presence kept the ghouls and vampires at bay.

I felt happy. It was the kind of happiness that comes from being rescued or from something awful coming to an end.

I turned toward my hostage-taker and folded my arms around him. I rested my head against his white cotton shirt, my monkey dangling from my hand. I felt immeasurable love for him. I wanted him with all my being, I wanted him more than seemed humanly possible. I'd never been truly in love, but now that it had happened, there was no question about it—what I was feeling was love. Whatever I'd felt in the past—guys I'd thought were cute or wished I was dating—all that was a kid's infatuation compared to this.

I knew there was a good reason he hadn't been able to see

me, and I was afraid for him. Yes, he'd done something incredibly stupid and wrong, but he did it because he thought it was the right thing.

"I love you, I love you," I murmured.

My hostage-taker didn't return my hug, but he didn't push me away. I was too desperate.

"Definitely the embrace of an athlete," he said.

"Former athlete," I corrected him. But he was the one who felt strong and sturdy against my body, and for a moment it seemed to me that I couldn't tell us apart; I couldn't tell where his body ended and mine began. I wanted his strength to flow into me and for my love to flow into him. My face was pressed against his chest, and I could hear his heart beating under his shirt. It made him seem unbearably vulnerable.

"I'm sorry I bit you," I said.

"Let's sit down," he said finally and carefully extricated himself from my grasp. We sat on the ground and I flattened my hand on the uneven surface. The earth was as alive as I was, and I was sure it could feel me as intensely as I felt it.

"I couldn't come before," he said. "I would have, but it wasn't possible."

"I was sure you'd been killed. And that stupid can opener broke."

"Yes, I saw. I'm very sorry. I'll bring a new one that won't break, but this won't happen again, I promise."

"How much longer will I be here?"

"I don't know."

"What about school?"

"I'm sure they'll make allowances. I'm supposed to transmit a message from your high school in fact."

"Really?"

"Yes."

"Why didn't you?"

"Because it's a charade," he said, pronouncing the word so it rhymed with *fraud*.

"What do you mean, charade?" I asked, imitating his pronunciation of the word.

"Messages sent to you, by all sorts of groups, jumping on the opportunity to exploit the situation. Maybe not your high school, but there's politics involved in almost everything else."

"Do you hate Americans?" I had to clear away obstacles to how I felt about him, I had to know that he was who I thought he was. I wouldn't be able to love him if he was full of blind hatred.

But he said, as I knew he would, "How can I hate people I don't know?"

"What about your friend?"

"What happened had nothing to do with politics. It was about power. Weak people can't resist the seduction of power, and they can't resist abusing it."

"You have power over me, too," I said.

He didn't answer. He seemed very tired suddenly.

I stopped talking. Maybe he'd fall asleep and I'd be able to stay outdoors longer. I realized that I no longer wanted to escape. If I escaped now, he'd be caught.

He read my mind. "We can't remain out here for too long.

These woods aren't part of the property."

"Just a few more minutes. My monkey needs the fresh air."

"Have you given him a name?"

"Abducted monkeys don't get to have names. They become anonymous, just like me."

"You're far from anonymous," he said.

"I don't know what I would have done without him." I planted a loud kiss on my monkey's head. "Where did you find him?"

"Just a kiosk. I was lucky to spot him in my rush."

"It's funny," I mused. "When I thought you weren't coming, the most ordinary things became demonic. Music, my own voice, a tube of toothpaste. I fell into a sort of madness— ordinary things were transformed into something grotesque or evil. But what if the way we see things, as harmless and safe, is just as arbitrary? What if it's only more practical to see the world as neutral, and that's why the people who experience a harmless world are the normal ones?"

"We should be getting back."

"Just five more minutes," I begged. "If I were a botanist, maybe I could figure out where I was according to the type of trees. But I don't want to know. I'm glad I can't identify them."

"So am I."

"I feel like Pirate Jenny, with this black floppy hat. Do you know that play? *The Threepenny Opera?*"

"Yes."

"We put it on last year at my high school. Guess who I was. You'll never guess. Mack the Knife! It feels like a hundred years ago. *When we encounter / A different sort of person / Our dispositions worsen,*" I sang. "*We squish them up and feed them / To lions.* Don't worry, I didn't sing alone, there was a chorus and we sang together."

"Your boyfriend mentioned that play."

"My boyfriend? I don't have a boyfriend!"

"Chad, I think his name is."

"Chad! We only had two dates, and they were a disaster. Is he going around telling people he's my boyfriend?"

"I think there was some dispute ... I didn't follow it."

"I can't believe that creep is saying he's my boyfriend. I've lost control not only of my life but of my entire past. And it's all your fault. I nearly lost my mind because of you. You're lucky I didn't try to kill myself."

"You're a very strong person."

"You need strong nerves in gymnastics. But I went round the bend while you were gone. Oh my God!" I cried out.

"What is it?"

"Oh God, my face! I totally forgot!" I touched my face and felt the streaks of lipstick on my cheeks. I threw my monkey at my hostage-taker and ran back to the warehouse. He followed me inside and this time he locked the door.

I knew when I came out of the bathroom that my face was red, and not only from being scrubbed.

"There's nothing unusual about face painting," he said.

"I don't want to talk about it," I muttered.

I looked through the food he'd brought and helped myself to bits of everything: triangles made of baked dough and stuffed with cottage cheese, a spiced rice dish, salad, cous-cous, baklava. He sat at the table and watched me. He looked completely exhausted.

"Why don't you lie down?" I suggested. "I promise I won't stab you in your sleep."

He hesitated, but his fatigue won out. "Maybe just for a few minutes," he said.

He stretched out on the bed, placed his hands on his chest, and closed his eyes. I put a CD in the player—I'd labeled all the disks by now—and "Heart Skipped a Beat" filled the room.

I went over to him, sat cross-legged by his side, and gazed at his face. He opened his eyes and they interlocked with mine. He seemed to be looking at me with less reserve than usual.

I began to run my fingers gently along his arm. He pushed my hand away, but instead of letting go he held on to it. He didn't just clasp my hand in his, thumb over knuckles; he interlaced his fingers with mine. The gesture made me deliriously happy. I felt as if his entire body had encased me; I felt loved and protected.

I leaned down and brushed my lips against his. To my amazement he slid his tongue into my mouth. But the kiss only lasted a second or two. He threw himself back abruptly, sat up, and even more surprisingly, covered his face with both his hands. He'd never shown me that side of him—a side that was not in complete control of the situation.

I sat up too and stared at him. He finally uncovered his face but he wouldn't look at me. "I have to go," he said.

"No, no!" I cried out. "I can't be alone again, not yet. I'm too scared—I'll go crazy if I you leave. We don't even have to speak …" My voice trailed off.

"I need you to promise to respect the line between us."

What line? I thought. I had a sudden image of the chalk border my friend Belinda and her sister drew on the floor of their bedroom, to mark their sides of the room, and it made me smile.

"I promise," I said.

I removed my jeans and slid in between my hostage-taker and the wall. I relaxed for the first time since I'd been left alone; I felt my body unwinding muscle by muscle. I was more tired than I'd realized, and before long I was asleep.

I woke up an hour later. My hostage-taker was still asleep, but he'd turned over on his side, and his arm was draped around my waist. His body felt warm and lovely against my back.

Our bodies are a perfect fit, I thought drowsily. I knew he must have moved toward me in his sleep. Probably he was dreaming that we were ordinary people in ordinary circum-stances and that it was okay to drape his arm around my waist.

Or maybe it wasn't even me in the dream. Maybe it was some girlfriend of his. Why not, after all? I lay very still, not daring to move. Eventually I drifted off again. When I woke, he was gone.

Angie Shaw trying not to lose my cool but really getting tired of all these scenarios people are coming up with for Chloe. We don't know how she's being treated, what's the point of imagining sick stuff? I mean, there's enough to worry about as it is without all that negativity. Yes she's a virgin. So what? If anything's happening to her it doesn't make a difference if she is or isn't. And the group might be psychos but they might not be. No one knows who they are. Even if they're a cult, not all cults are like Manson. Some cults they just sit around and meditate. We just DON'T KNOW. So please everyone stop speculating.

16 minutes ago   Comment   Like   Wall-to-wall

 Kimmy Xuan yeah, my favorite is that she's sleeping in a coffin. So random. I personally don't think the hostage takers are off the wall because look at their demands. They've studied all the cases, they know the laws, the name is probably to throw people off track. So I agree, we can't know anything and people have to stop acting as if Chloe is a character in a movie or something. I just wish there was more we could do.

11 minutes ago   Comment   Like   Wall-to-wall

 Angie Shaw Thanks, Kimmy. I was thinking one thing we can do is maybe volunteer at Happy Sprites. Chloe's mom must be up to her ears trying to keep things going smoothly there and doing all the work for Chloe at the same time. So if anyone has some time to hang out at the reception desk and keep an eye on things, I'm sure she'd be eternally grateful.

9 minutes ago   Comment   Like   Wall-to-wall

CHAPTER 15

Luckily, I wasn't on my own for long. I didn't feel up to an entire day by myself; I was sure the irrational terror I'd experienced was still lurking in the shadows, ready to creep back into my thoughts. But my hostage-taker returned just before noon.

I was lying on the bed, listening to Coldplay and daydreaming about my hostage-taker, about our kiss. I kept wondering whether he had a girlfriend. I felt I had to know. I had to know or I'd die.

When I heard the key in the lock I jumped up and ran to the door. I was both excited and nervous; I suddenly felt a little shy.

"Do you want tea?" he asked, as if nothing had happened between us, as if he hadn't kissed me, really kissed me, for a few seconds, and then held me as we slept.

He opened the fridge door and put away the containers he'd brought. He always lined things up neatly in the fridge; I'd never known anyone who did that with food.

"Do you have a girlfriend?" I blurted out.

He didn't answer. I was still wearing the T-shirt I wore for sleep—his T-shirt. I went to the bathroom and pulled on my jeans and purple sleeveless top. I was getting really and truly bored with wearing the same thing day in, day out. Using my all-purpose compact mirror, I put on lip gloss and my mauve eye shadow.

"How do I look?" I asked him, when I emerged from the saloon doors.

"You look well rested."

"Are you ... religious?"

He stared at me, but I couldn't decipher the look in his eyes. Finally he said, "No."

"So ... like ... it isn't against your religion or anything to date?"

Again he seemed to be looking at me in a complicated way. I went over to his chair, sat down on his lap, and started kissing him lightly on the lips. I couldn't stop myself; he had the most irresistible mouth I'd ever seen. Appropriately, "Speed of Sound" was playing. I too was wondering—how long would it take before he let me in?

He kissed me back for a second, his lips responding instinctively to mine. I wanted us to merge into one; my whole being was drawn to him as if magnetically.

I don't know whether we would have gone on kissing for more than a few seconds had I not touched him. My hands were on the arms of the chair; instinctively I moved them to his shoulders. My need to touch him was overwhelming; it was a physical craving like thirst or hunger. I was holding back, in fact, because I wanted to run my fingers through his hair, press him to me as hard as I could.

But as soon as my hands settled on his shoulders, he rose from the chair and pushed me away.

"I'm sorry," I said. "I just want to feel close to someone. The last time someone touched me was to hurt me. It made me feel like I was nothing. That I wasn't a person. I just want to replace that memory, I want to erase it."

"This is not the way to erase anything," he said. He sat back down, but he pulled his chair away from the table, as if for safety. His body was wary, alert. "I don't want to see you emotionally unbalanced."

"What can be more unbalancing than loving someone who doesn't love you back!"

"I'm not someone you would ever have chosen in ordinary circumstances."

"That's not true," I protested. "If I'd met you, I would have chosen you. It's your personality I love. It's you."

And you liked when I kissed you, I thought. I was sure of it. Both times he'd kissed me back for a few seconds. His body was going in one direction, his mind in another.

"You're bored," he insisted, "with nothing to occupy you and no one else in your life right now."

"You couldn't be more wrong," I replied.

"I'd like to change the direction of this conversation."

"Okay, okay, we won't talk about it." I opened the fridge door and took out one of the containers he'd stacked on the shelves.

"Oh goody, rice pudding. Where did you learn how to cook? You're so good at it."

"I brought a chessboard," he told me. "It said in the paper you used to play with your grandfather."

"God, that was years and years ago! I don't even know if I remember the basics. Anyhow, I was a horrible player."

"I could remind you."

He set up the board and I watched his slender fingers arrange the pieces as he went over the rules.

"It's coming back," I said. "You'll have to remove your queen, otherwise you'll win in two moves. That's what my granddad did. You'll win in two moves anyway, but you'll have a bigger sense of accomplishment if you do it without your queen."

We began to play, but we were both unfocused and kept blundering.

"I guess you have a lot on your mind," I said, wishing I knew everything about him. In the beginning I'd wanted to know what he was like so I'd know whether I was safe. Now I wanted to know more so we'd be closer.

"You could say that."

I almost apologized, but I caught myself and laughed. "I almost apologized to you! But it's your fault. You've really got yourself into a mess now. How could you do something so incredibly stupid?"

"Check," he said.

I couldn't be bothered saving my king. I got up and put on one of the compilation CDs. "Young Folk" came on and I began to dance. My hostage-taker watched me in his usual indecipherable way.

"You never smile," I teased as I danced. "Or maybe you just don't smile here. Maybe you smile when you're with your friends. Come, dance with me." I tried to pull him up.

He sighed. It was the first time I'd heard him sigh. He got up, took his things, and left the warehouse without looking at me. I heard the key turn on the outside. It occurred to me that he never said hello or goodbye. He never smiled and he never said hello or goodbye.

Chloe Mills False Alarm Leads to Rescue

A tip from a concerned citizen in a Milan neighborhood led to the rescue of a kidnapped girl, 9, who had been reported missing after not arriving home from school yesterday.

The citizen, who has not been identified by name, was convinced she had discovered the place where Chloe Mills was being held captive. The U.S. teenager was taken hostage earlier this summer while working in Greece.

It has been surmised that Chloe may have been taken from Greece to Italy by boat. Citizens in both Italy and Greece have been asked to report anything suspicious, with an Interpol website listing warning signals to watch out for.

As a result of increased vigilance, a woman notified police of suspicious events at a house in her neighborhood.

The police surrounded the house and discovered not Chloe, but another kidnapping victim. The girl was returned safely to tearful parents. Two arrests have been made.

Allegra Mills, Chloe's mother, said, "I know Chloe would be glad to know that awareness of her plight led to the rescue of this poor girl."

POST REPORT

CHAPTER 16

I dreamed I was trying to hug my hostage-taker, but when I touched him I realized it wasn't him, it was a hologram he'd left for me in the warehouse so I wouldn't feel alone. My monkey, on the other hand, was alive—he was jumping around and trying to mime something, but I couldn't tell what it was he was trying to tell me. I felt frustrated and confused in the dream, and I was relieved when I woke up, though my reality wasn't much better.

I was very restless. I tried to exercise: I had by now revived my walkovers, cartwheels, handstands, and even some back handsprings. My hostage-taker had brought me a mat, but it was old and scruffy and smelled of stale peanuts. I wondered where he'd found it.

I showered out of boredom and then wrote in my notebook. Recording our conversation reminded me of Chad. What else had he told the press? I hoped Angie would set the record straight.

We'd met at one of Angie's pool parties. He asked me on a date and I agreed—mostly because I couldn't think of an excuse on the spot. The date wasn't memorable until he tried to kiss me in the car. The gesture felt imposed and insincere, as if he was trying to prove something. He was offended when I moved away. "So what they say about you is right," he snapped. "They call you the Ice Queen behind your back."

The next day he texted an apology. He confessed he'd invented the Ice Queen accusation to save his wounded pride, and he begged for a second chance.

Our second date was not much better. We went to an exhibit about natural disasters that he wanted to see. Then we sat at the fountain and had ice cream. He kept saying, "It's a dog eat dog world." So annoying! Dogs don't in fact eat other dogs, if you want to be literal about it, and that's what I finally told him. Things went downhill from there. He didn't call me again, and luckily I didn't run into him.

Now, on the basis of two meaningless dates, he was telling everyone that we were going out. Was he trying to get attention or revenge?

Chad was my only official date. Usually I just hung out with people at parties or wherever. In the past year I'd come across a few guys I liked, but nothing came of it. Mom said I was afraid of forming attachments because of Dad's sudden death. She also said that when I met the right man I'd get over my fear of being deserted.

Well, the right man had finally come along, through an incredible twist of fate. Unfortunately, he was a criminal who was now wanted internationally.

I spent the day reading a book called *Dreams of Self*. It was about how we're programmed to act the way we do by millions of years of adaptation. We think our emotions and thoughts make us who we are, but according to the author, it's all about survival mechanisms.

Nothing could be that simple. If it were, we'd all be exactly the same. Instead, we were so different that it was hard to find anyone who was on your wavelength. We might be programmed in a general sort of way, but the details had to have more complicated reasons.

I wondered whether my hostage-taker felt the way I had felt when Chad tried to kiss me—that I was just trying to prove something. Maybe he wasn't attracted to me. But he did kiss me back for a second.

I trusted him now. That's what it came down to. I tried to remember when I'd started trusting him. Maybe it was when he lay down on my bed and fell asleep. Seeing him lying there, vulnerable and unprotected, made me certain that he was telling me the truth. And my certainty made me happy.

Happiness is not only an outcome of love, I realized. It's a sign of love. It's the way you know that you love someone—you can tell by the way that person makes you feel. It's as simple as that.

So it wasn't only him I trusted—it was my instincts. If I felt that way about him, it meant he was trustworthy.

Everything he had done and said was consistent. He wanted to release a prisoner he felt was innocent. He'd chosen a crazy, illegal way to do it, but he wasn't violent. He was furious that the other guy had hurt me, and he had probably cut off all contact with him.

Did he work in a hospital? Maybe he was even a doctor—he wasn't too young to be an intern. But he didn't act like a doctor, somehow. More likely he'd trained as a paramedic or something like that.

The day crawled by in slow motion. When I finally heard the key in the lock, my heart began to pound with excitement.

"I thought about you all day," I said as soon as he walked in. "I couldn't wait for you to come."

"Shall we sit in the sun for a short while?" he asked.

"Indeed, shall we?" I replied in my fake British accent.

We brought out the chairs and sat in the sun, side by side, as if we were two ordinary people.

"Are you sure it's safe to sit out here?" I asked. The thought of storm troopers crashing into the warehouse with machine-guns horrified me.

"Yes, it's safe."

"What about the ... other man? How can you trust him not to do anything stupid?"

He didn't answer, but he turned his head to look at me. I couldn't interpret his look.

"If it's so safe, why am I wearing a hat?"

"In case someone sees us from the woods. It's unlikely, though."

"I'm torn," I said. "I don't want to take a risk, even a tiny one, but I love it out here. I'm connecting to nature in a new way. My mom would be pleased. She's into all that stuff about being one with the world. What religion were you brought up with?"

I didn't expect an answer, but he surprised me. "My parents were secular, but the community was mostly Catholic."

It was strange, thinking of him as someone with parents, a family, maybe brothers and sisters. He'd seemed almost like an alien from another planet until now. I couldn't imagine him sitting around with friends at a café, for example. I couldn't imagine him as a kid. He was too somber, if that was the right word.

"Why me?" I asked. "Why did you choose me?"

"You were alone. You looked healthy. We'd heard you say you were from the United States."

"Heard me? When?"

"At the bus stop."

"You were there!?"

"Yes."

"I didn't see you."

"I know."

"Were you specifically looking for a woman?"

"Yes. I thought a woman might arouse more concern, and also wouldn't force us to be too aggressive. A man would think it his duty to resist continually."

"That's so sexist. You think all women are submissive?"

"Not at all. Women are resilient, with many resources men often lack. Women don't seem as interested in physical violence, however."

I pulled my floppy black hat down over my eyes and leaned my head back on the wall. "You obviously haven't met my biology teacher. All she does in her spare time is watch kung fu movies."

"I suppose we were fortunate to abduct you and not your biology teacher."

"I guess you had a good laugh when I said I was diabetic."

"People will say whatever they can to get out of a situation like that. I'd have been surprised if you hadn't said something along those lines."

"What if I'd lost it? I mean—I was pretty close to the

edge. You can't imagine what it's like to be so scared."

He looked away from me and shifted in his chair. I felt that he was on the verge of saying, *I don't need to imagine it.*

"Aren't you afraid that when you release me I'll describe this place?" I asked.

"You won't be able to direct anyone to me, or to this place," he said.

"Were you nervous, when you took me?"

"I have good control."

I laughed. "Yes, I can see that! You never smile, you never show any feeling at all. It's weird. Your eyes are expressive, but not the rest of your face. Your eyes and your body."

I felt antsy; I wanted to move around, take a walk—even if only to the forest and back. I got up from my chair, did a few stretches, touched my toes. Then I did a cartwheel, before he had a chance to stop me. My hat fell off, but I quickly replaced it.

"I'd prefer it if you sat quietly," he said.

"Sorry," I said. I didn't want him to change his mind about letting me go out. "You don't know how lucky you are that you didn't end up with Angie! It would serve you right if you'd captured Angie instead of me. You would have had your hands full."

"I'm sure I would have managed."

"You don't know Angie. For one thing, she's phobic about cockroaches—or any insect, for that matter. She would have been in a state of permanent hysteria—you'd have had to find a whole different location for her. And even if you gave her all the art supplies in the world, she'd never stop crying and moaning. You would have regretted the day you ever came up with this crazy idea."

I almost managed to get a smile out of him. I realized how triumphant that would have made me—as if I'd won some sort of victory. His detachment gave him power over me.

But he only tilted his head. His eyes were amused, and even his hands seemed amused, but he stopped short of actually smiling.

"I'm thinking of letting my hair grow. Do you think long hair would suit me?"

"Yes, I think so."

"You actually have an opinion about my appearance!" I shrieked. "I'm not just a hostage to you!"

"Please keep your voice down. You were never just a hostage," he said.

"The minute you take someone hostage, they become just a hostage. You can be in denial about that, if you want."

My hostage-taker shut his eyes and leaned his head on the wall. He seemed to be half asleep.

I didn't mind; it was enough to be out in the sun together. "I love you, I love you," I whispered under my hat, but I couldn't tell whether he'd heard.

Angie Shaw's first day of school was a nightmare. I kept crying all the time, police had to be called in to keep away media, but kids kept taking pics and recording everything, probably to sell to the press. Where is the no-gadget policy when you need it? People were so insensitive, as if it's all a joke and not real and just some fake story. As if Chloe's on vacation somewhere instead of God knows where and God knows with what sort of people. Lots of horrible jokes too. I couldn't believe it. I still can't believe it. Don't want to go back to school tomorrow. And then being there without Chloe for the first time ever, so depressing. Help!!!

15 minutes ago   Comment   Like   Wall-to-wall

Belinda Lyons yeah I couldn't believe it either. I think there's going to be an assembly about it tomorrow, that's the rumor. Hopefully that'll help. Hard to believe how nasty some kids are. People have already posted their videos all over the place. Interviews with teachers, everything.

13 minutes ago   Comment   Like   Wall-to-wall

Angie Shaw Thanks Belinda, but I realized I don't care about myself. Yeah my day sucked, but I don't care as long as Chloe comes back. What's a few comments compared to what she's going through. I keep thinking of all the hostages who've been executed, it's so horrible. I wonder if Patty Hearst can come and talk to our school. She's been so supportive. One thing I know about Chloe, she won't get brainwashed. I just really miss her. I feel her not being there so much more now that school's started. Don't know what I'd do without all of you guys. The worst thing is how guilty I feel when I have ice cream or pizza or take a long bath … enjoying stuff while Chloe suffers. I like what Chloe's mom said—Two people suffering instead of one doesn't improve the world. And it's looking good, the legal team is doing a fantastic job!

7 minutes ago   Comment   Like   Wall-to-wall

CHAPTER 17

No plan is foolproof. Not in films, and not in real life. I was sitting on my bed with the Italian textbook when I heard voices outside the warehouse.

I thought at first that I was imagining things. But then the sounds grew louder: laughter, talking, whispering. Though I didn't know what language was being spoken, I was sure the excited, high-pitched voices came from kids—mostly boys, as far as I could tell, about ten or eleven years old.

I was relieved that they were only kids, but I still had to be careful not to let them know I was there. I read quietly on my bed, enjoying the chatter and laughter, until all at once the sounds stopped. They'd gone.

It was only by luck that I hadn't had my music on. But even if they'd heard it, they wouldn't have known who was inside the warehouse.

It was nearly dark when my hostage-taker arrived. He said as soon as he entered, "There was someone here. I found cigarette butts and an empty can outside."

"Yes, some kids. At least, they sounded like kids. Don't worry, I was careful. Lucky the music wasn't on."

He froze when I said that. He didn't move at all. He just stood there and stared at me.

"I told you I don't want you to get caught," I said. "I don't want you to be killed, obviously, or even to go to jail."

He went on staring at me.

"Don't stare at me like that," I said. "It's creeping me out."

"You didn't call for help?" he asked finally.

"No, of course not."

"Why?"

"I love you. And I don't think you deserve to go to prison. You've broken the law, of course, and what you're doing is wrong, but I don't want you to be found. Let's say I wanted to marry you one day," I heard myself saying. "It wouldn't be any fun if you were serving a life sentence."

He was barely listening. He said, "They must have climbed the fence, looking for a private place to smoke."

"They'll be back, in that case," I warned him.

"When were they here?"

"Around two in the afternoon."

He looked at me even more intently. He was deathly pale, and it scared me.

"You saved my life," he said evenly. "You had a chance to be free, and you didn't take it."

"If I were free I wouldn't see you again. That's too awful to think about."

He sat down and tried to regain his equanimity. He was very wound up.

His nervousness was making me nervous. "I don't seem to be making much progress in Italian," I said, trying to change the subject. "I have all this time, and I'm wasting it. I used to hate wasting time, but now I'm starting to see that it has its own appeal."

He didn't hear me. He was too preoccupied.

"Why don't you have some tea?" I suggested. "I'll make it

for a change." I looked inside the bags he'd brought. "Oh, lemon squares! My favorite, how did you know?"

"I'm sorry, I have to leave." He got up abruptly, went out, locked the door. I didn't hear him drive away. Maybe he had an escape route through a tunnel or under the floor of another warehouse, like in war movies. He'd probably considered all eventualities—except the simple one of a group of kids looking for a safe place to smoke.

I felt more alone than ever, after he'd gone. I couldn't really blame him for not trusting me—he had no way of knowing what I was thinking and feeling. But it was demoralizing all the same.

The only way to escape the lonely room was to sleep, but I wasn't tired. I paced, ate five lemon squares, had another shower, paced some more, tried to read. Finally I drifted off, but it was a light sleep, and I woke up as soon as I heard the key in the door.

"You're back! Were you hiding all this time?"

He looked at me for a few seconds as if I'd changed, as if something was different about me. But what had changed, of course, was him. I could see it in his eyes. He finally trusted me.

He plugged in the kettle. "I want to thank you," he said. "You sacrificed your freedom for me."

"It wasn't a sacrifice."

He made tea for me and coffee for himself. He was still wound up, but in a different way. His face was less impassive, though probably only I would have noticed it.

"Your body's telling me something," I said.

"My body?"

"Yes. You don't have an expressive face, but you have an expressive body. Sometimes I can read it."

"I'm sure it's your imagination."

"Oh, no! Not at all. Your body says everything you don't say with your face."

"What is it saying now?"

"I'm not sure. No, that's a lie. I am sure, but I'm not allowed to say. But I'll say it anyhow because I have nothing to lose. That's the definition of desperation, isn't it?"

"Yes."

"What I'm reading in your body is that you like me."

"Yes, I like you very much," he replied casually, trying to change the meaning of what I'd said. "You're a beautiful person."

I felt a rush of happiness coursing through me when he said that. No compliment had ever meant anything, compared to this.

Of course he didn't know about my obsessive side, the side that drove people crazy. But it seemed to me that I was changing.

"I think my personality is changing a bit," I told him.

"Hard experiences always change us, for better or for worse. Sometimes both."

"I sometimes felt when I was growing up that I was the parent and Mom was the kid. I don't mean in a bad way. It's just that Mom was the one who believed in being sponta- neous, taking chances, enjoying life. I was the opposite. I was always checking the time to make sure we weren't late, I kept a list on the fridge of things we had to buy, and if we were going out I wanted to make sure we knew the way. I don't think Mom would have let me go into gymnastics if anyone there had turned it into boot camp. But the club I joined was run by the sweetest, funniest coach, Luanne. She wore her hair in a braid that reached down to her waist, and she sang along to country and western music while we trained. But anyhow, finally she retired. We all cried on her last day.

"It wasn't the same after that. The coach who took over was nice too, but much more ambitious. Mom said ambition was about something outside of you, something that didn't even exist. Whatever. The real reason I quit was that I was getting sick of giving up sixteen hours of my life every week. I wanted a normal life."

I knew I was rambling. It was excitement. The way he was looking at me made me hyper and also happy, and being happy made me talkative. I wanted to be close to him, I wanted him to know me better, now that he knew I loved him. I went on, "I take more after my father, he was a biologist. He died when he was only thirty-seven—he had a heart defect ... So, do you have to contact all your revolutionary friends now and tell them about the close call? Do you guys have a name, by the way? You know, like the Gourmet Liberation Front, or something? Working to release prisoners who've been convicted of withholding recipes ... Sorry. I don't mean to make fun of you."

"Jokes are allowed by the GLF."

"If the police had come, would you have shot at them?"

"I don't own a weapon."

I laughed. "You're joking!"

"No."

"You studied martial arts, though," I said, remembering our fight in the forest. "You really don't have a gun?" I asked.

"There wouldn't be any point. If I'm caught, I'm caught."

"You could hold the gun to my head and pretend you're going to kill me," I suggested.

"It's a good thing we have films to give us valuable information," he said.

"So … I could have escaped right there in the limo?"

"I don't think so. I would have found a way to hold on to you."

"I was sure I'd be killed if I didn't cooperate."

"We were counting on that."

"Well, it was worth being terrified out of my skull. It was worth everything, even … It was worth it, to find you. I knew you wouldn't shoot at the police. Do you think it's wrong to kill someone for the greater good?" I asked.

"Is this a test?" Absently, he cut off a piece of lemon square with a fork, but he didn't eat it.

"Well, do you?" I insisted.

"You don't kill innocent people to help humanity. It's a contradiction in terms. At least that's my view."

"But what about a dictator, for example?"

"That would not be an innocent civilian," he replied.

"So you might believe in assassinating someone."

"If you assassinate one person, someone else will just take over. Even if they'd succeeded in killing Hitler, probably Goebbels would have taken his place, though it would have been worth a try."

"What about in a war? I mean, when you bomb a city, you kill innocent people, but sometimes it's the only way to win a war."

"Is it?"

"I don't know," I said.

"It would be good to prevent war in the first place."

"Well, no one would argue with that! But it's unrealistic. There are terrible people in this world. And sometimes they have power."

"Yes, that's true," he said. "Anyhow, bombing a city is a war crime."

"You're one to talk about crimes! Taking me hostage is a major crime."

"Yes, but maybe not as serious as burning infants to death."

"You think you know everything."

All at once, out of the blue, I wondered whether the sadistic man who had nearly killed me was dead.

I don't know what made me think it at that moment— whether it was his tone of voice or his eyes or his body. Angie believed that images sometimes passed from one person's brain to another. Or maybe there had been lots of clues that I'd noticed only subconsciously, and that had suddenly come to the surface.

He seemed to know what I was thinking, but he didn't ask me what was wrong, even though I was suddenly staring at him.

"Did you kill him?" I asked. I was afraid of his answer. I had no idea how I'd feel if he said yes. I hated the man who had hurt me, I wanted him dead, but I didn't want to be in love with someone who was capable of murder.

There was a long silence. Then he said, "Yes, in a way."

"What does that mean?"

"He was an addict. We gave him a huge amount of money and he bought a huge amount of heroin. He died of an overdose."

My reaction took me by surprise. I began to cry. "I'm glad," I said. "I'm glad he's dead. Of course if you weren't a criminal yourself, you could have had him arrested." I began pounding my leg with my fist.

"Chloe." I was so startled to hear my name that my arm froze in mid-air. He had never said my name before. "It's not your responsibility. There's a long and complicated story behind this, one that started many years ago. Sometimes you try to save people who don't want to be saved. And you finally realize that they'll push you and push you until they get what they want."

"Is that why you were away for so long that time?"

"No, that was something else. He was already dead by then."

"I feel so weird. As if the world's tilting a little."

"Someone once told me a joke," he said. "'I'd like to be a

pacifist, but people keep getting in the way.' I made a decision to fight for my friend in prison. It was a deliberate decision. It isn't the only way—it's just something I decided."

"But how can you trust your judgment?" I protested. "How can one person decide which laws count and which ones don't? Laws have to be decided on collectively, by a society."

"Sometimes breaking the law is just the best of several bad options. Sometimes a situation is so desperate that you can't go by the rules."

"If you were a law-abiding citizen you wouldn't get into desperate situations in the first place," I pointed out.

He paused, then said, "It's just beyond belief, what power does to some people. It acts as a sort of drug. The stupider the person, the more likely it is that having power will corrupt them."

"I saw that happen once," I said. "I never thought of it that way, I never thought of it as a power thing. But I used to be in the student council at school, and one time this shy, friendly girl got to chair a meeting. We were trying to give everyone a chance to chair, and it was her turn. We couldn't believe the personality transformation … she turned into an army general, putting everyone down, bossing people in this totally inappropriate way—it was weird. I guess that's what it was—power. She really did act like she was on something."

He wasn't listening to me. He was thinking about something else, something that happened a long time ago. I could tell by the faraway look in his eyes.

The man who'd hurt me seemed human to me for the

first time. It was safe to think of him as human now that he was dead. Now that I didn't have to be afraid of him.

"The writer Emile Zola thought guilt haunts you, but he was wrong. Have you read him?"

I shook my head.

"He has this woman and her lover killing the woman's sickly, selfish husband," he said. "After they do it, they're haunted by guilt and by the horror of it, and it destroys their lives. But it's not like that. You're sick the first few days, and then it fades."

"Yeah, that writer is way off," I said. "Sociopaths never feel guilty at all. This girl who used to go to my school, Rik— every day she had a few people in tears, otherwise her life just wasn't worth living. I'm sure she'll never feel guilt. She loved who she was."

He seemed to be considering what he could and couldn't say. He didn't usually come across as undecided, but for once I could sense his uncertainty.

"Can you open the door, please?" I asked.

"You can open it yourself," he said, and I saw that the door wasn't locked. I stepped out into the dark and my hostage-taker followed me. It was a hot, moonless night and I could see millions of stars against the vast black sky.

I looked up at the starry sky and said, "Good-bye, messed-up person. If there's an afterlife, I hope you get a second chance there. Also, I guess I forgive you, even though you hurt me a lot. And tried to make me feel like I was a person who deserved to be hated, or like no person at all. Anyway, I forgive you. And my hostage-taker forgives you too, though it's hard for him to say it now."

My hostage-taker placed his arm around my shoulders. It was so unexpected and comforting that I didn't dare breathe.

"How do you keep people off the property?" I asked.

"I won't have to. You're going to be moving to another location."

"When?" I asked.

"In a few hours. I'm just waiting for the vehicle."

"Another warehouse?"

"No, a room. Smaller, but you'll have a bath."

"How? How will you move me?"

"You'll find out soon enough."

"What if you're caught on the way?"

He led me back inside and dropped his arm from my shoulder. What if he never touched me again? Maybe holding me had only been a friendly gesture, a way of showing gratitude or consoling me for the bad news.

He took out the white wine and filled two glasses. He handed me a glass and sat down at the table with his.

"I hope this teaches you a lesson," I said primly. "No matter how carefully you plan, things can go wrong."

"That's true enough."

"Don't you see? Someone might have seen me getting on the plane. Or coming off the plane—I was asleep so I don't know how you managed to do that inconspicuously. That guy—the addict—he might have told someone. You're risking your life, apart from everything else."

It felt good, lecturing him. I wanted to shake him out of his stubbornness. "When you release me, I'm going to say that you gave me a choice of staying or leaving right on the first day. And that I stayed here of my own free will."

"We'll talk about that another time."

I looked down at the floor and jiggled my legs nervously. "Maybe in a few months, when everyone's forgotten about me, we can meet, as if by chance—like at a party or something."

He shook his head. "It's not possible. Once you go home, we won't be able to meet again, ever."

The thought of never seeing him again made me desperate. "Is it because you don't have feelings for me? Is that why we can't meet again?"

"It's because it's too dangerous. You'll be followed for a long time. And I have many things I need to do. I haven't set out to have an ordinary life."

"Have you ever been married?" I asked.

"No. That's not where I'm headed."

"You can change where you're headed," I persisted.

"I don't want to change. By the way, I need from you the location of your mother's secret hiding place. To prove you're alive."

"My mother's secret hiding place? She doesn't have one … Oh! She means up in the attic. Behind the *Birth of Venus* poster. I guess she'll have to find a new hiding place now."

"Thank you."

"Tell me how you feel about me," I pleaded. "If you tell me you can never love me I won't bring up the subject again, I promise."

He paused and seemed to be considering his answer. "I do have feelings for you," he admitted finally. "But they're irrelevant."

"Do you love me?"

"I guess you'd call it love."

His words were like a sweet, warm mantle falling from the sky and folding me inside it. I felt a flush rising to my face as I smiled at him. I wanted his expression to confirm what he'd just said, but his arms were crossed in front of his chest and I couldn't read him at all.

"What would *you* call it?" I asked.

"Feelings I'm trying not to have."

I felt my heart brimming over with joy. I didn't even know it was possible to be so happy. "I knew it!" I exclaimed. "I knew you loved me, I felt it."

"You'll change your mind once you're free. You'll start to understand that your attraction to me is nothing but a trick of the mind, a way to make the captivity bearable."

I was frustrated and annoyed by his refusal to believe me. But I laughed and said, "You have very low self-esteem, you know. You don't think I can really love you for yourself?"

"There's no way to tell, and we won't have a chance to find out, because our paths are going to separate. But you've become part of my history, a part I'll never forget."

"I'm not going to let you go. I'm going to refuse to leave. I can be quite stubborn," I informed him.

"If you refuse to leave, I'll get caught."

"I don't want to talk about this anymore."

"We'll be moving you in a few hours. You might want to get some sleep."

For a split second I was afraid. Afraid he was going to kill me. My fear shocked and embarrassed me. He saw both my fear and the embarrassment that followed.

"I'd be afraid too," he said.

"I'm not afraid of you. I love you. I've just seen too many Hollywood movies."

"I'm not going to harm you. But you're going to be uncomfortable for a short while. I'd give you something to make it easier, but I need you to be alert. I'm sorry to put you through this."

"Uncomfortable, how?"

"It'll be cramped. I hope you're not claustrophobic."

"If I wasn't before, I am now. Anyone would be, locked up like this. Anyhow, I'm way too hyper to sleep."

"I have to go get things ready. I'll be back before sunrise."

He left without bothering to lock the door.

Eight-Year-Old Raises $800,000 for Chloe Mills

An eight-year-old girl in U.S. hostage Chloe Mills' hometown of Chicago has raised an astonishing $800,000 for the Free Chloe Campaign by charging $5 for each view of a video in which she sings a song she wrote for the teenage hostage.

The talented young singer, Erika Elie, is a former winner on the popular television show "Spot the Starling."

The money is a boost for the campaign, which has had to hire a team of legal experts to assess and advance the demands of the abductors.

Yesterday a question that only Chloe can answer was sent to the abductors, who call themselves Children of Lord Ruthven, to ascertain that Chloe is alive. No information is available on the means the abductors are using to communicate their demands.

POST REPORT

CHAPTER 18

I did manage to get back to sleep, though bad dreams kept me tossing and turning. I dreamed I was clinging to a giant turtle, trying to hold on to him while he swam across a poisonous lake. I kept slipping because there was nothing to hold on to—if I held on to his neck, I'd choke him, and we'd both fall into the deadly water and die. The dream seemed to go on forever; even when I half woke it pulled me back.

At one point I thought I heard voices outside—one I recognized as my hostage-taker's but the other sounded like the voice of the addict. I knew it couldn't be him, I knew he was dead, but I felt a lightning bolt of terror. In a flash, it all came back to me. He'd shouted at me the whole time he was in the warehouse—American this, American that. As if everything that was wrong with the world was personally my fault. Each time he dunked me it was for another crime I was supposedly responsible for.

Then the voices died out and I realized they too had been part of my dream.

My hostage-taker returned just before dawn. He was pushing a trolley with a beautiful antique chest. I understood immediately; I was to hide inside the chest. It shocked me, somehow, and made me feel vaguely nauseous.

"Creepy," I said. "How long will it take?"

"About two hours."

I clasped myself protectively. "Good thing I'm flexible. What can I take with me?"

"You'll have everything you need there," he said.

"What about my notebooks? And the books?"

"I'll bring you those things later."

"So just me and my monkey?"

"Yes."

"An iPod would have been nice ... How will I breathe?"

"See here—I've taped slivers of wood to the corners. They'll keep the lid from closing all the way."

"When do we leave?"

"Now. Here's a bottle of water and some snacks. And a flashlight, if you want it." He handed me a baggie filled with crackers and small squares of cheese.

I packed a few essential items—watch, razor, lip gloss, eye shadow. Then, clutching my monkey in my arms and bracing myself, I climbed into the chest. There were blankets and two pillows inside for me to lie on. All the same, it was intensely oppressive.

"Oh, man," I said. "Now I know what those poor illegals feel like—the ones who try to sneak into countries in crates."

As the lid came down, I told myself not to be spoiled. It was only two hours, after all, and my hostage-taker was doing everything he could to make it as bearable as possible. I shouldn't be making such a fuss.

The trolley began to move. I lay on my side with my knees up and turned on the flashlight, but there was nothing to see. I couldn't even think of eating; the closed space and the bumpy ride were making me carsick.

We came to an abrupt stop. There were no sounds now

and no movement. The stillness and silence scared me. My old fears returned in spite of myself—what if I was being deserted, what if it had all been a trick? What if I was about to be buried in this box or dropped in a lake and drowned?

I knew I was being paranoid. A few seconds later the chest was tilted sideways onto what I assumed was a ramp leading to the back of a truck. I heard the thudding and banging of objects being moved around, followed by the sound of a door slamming shut.

I lifted the lid an inch or two and peeked out; it would be safe now. I saw that I was in the midst of a jumble of furniture: tables, desks, chairs, more chests.

The truck began to move and I felt slightly carsick again. I knew it was mostly nerves; I'd never suffered from motion sickness before, not even on the Dark Knight roller coaster at home.

I distracted myself by thinking about my hostage-taker: his expressive eyes and hands, his sense of humor, his refusal to take advantage of me. He was misguided but not in a hopeless way. He didn't even own a weapon. He'd done something wrong, but if he never did it again, there wasn't any reason to send him to prison. He wasn't dangerous. If anything, it was his idealism that had made him act so desperately.

How many people were helping him? Maybe there had only ever been the woman and the man who was dead. Maybe they were all related. What if the woman was his mother and the man was his brother? That would explain how he ended up trusting someone so unstable. Maybe they were a wealthy family and the prisoner they were trying to get released was part of the family. Maybe he was my hostage-taker's father! That would explain everything.

I'd find out when I got back. If the prisoner was my hostage-taker's father, I'd be able to track down my hostage-taker. The idea made me very happy, and I was finally able to relax in my bumpy box. I even munched on a cracker or two.

Suddenly the truck came to a stop. I knew we hadn't arrived because we'd only been traveling for about twenty minutes.

I heard traffic and I began to panic. The back of the truck creaked open. I froze, afraid even to breathe. What if I suddenly sneezed?

I heard a gruff voice speaking a foreign language, and my hostage-taker answering. *Oh God, please don't let us be caught*, I prayed. I'd seen this scene in so many movies. Sometimes people were caught and sometimes they weren't.

To my enormous relief, I heard laughter, the door slammed shut, and a few seconds later the truck continued on its way. *Thank you, God*, I whispered in the dark.

Free Chloe

To The People Holding Chloe, from Angie:
Please give Chloe this letter for her birthday.

Hi Chloe, I hope you get this message. We're all so worried about you and we're working really hard to get the demands met as much as possible. I hope your situation is okay and I'm so sorry I wasn't there to prevent it. You're still in the news every day and we've got a whole team of great lawyers working on the cases. I'm sending this from the free-chloe website—we're all praying that you come back safe and sound. Don't give up hope, and remember how much we love you. A million hugs.

CHAPTER 19

I heard the once-familiar sound of an automatic garage door going up and then coming down. It was lovely, hearing that sound again. It reminded me of families, car rides, civilization. Ordinary life.

My hostage-taker raised the lid of the trunk. "We're here," he said. "Are you all right?"

I nodded. My legs were stiff and wobbly from the ride and I needed help standing up. The garage was dark and bare and smelled of swimming pool chemicals. For no reason, I began to cry. It was just relief, I think. Relief that the move was over, relief that we hadn't been caught.

"Here's a blindfold," my hostage-taker said, ignoring my tears. "I'm going to lead you to the basement."

I nodded again and tied the black blindfold across my eyes. It was heavier and larger than the blindfold I'd had on when I was first taken, and I couldn't see a thing through it. My hostage-taker slid his arm around my waist and led me through a door. The sensation of soft carpeting under my feet startled me. Something as simple as walking on a carpet had become an alien experience.

We made our way down a flight of stairs. I held the railing with one hand and my hostage-taker's arm with the other. His arm felt strong and reliable, and I wished he'd lift me up and carry me.

The distance from the bottom of the stairs to my room suggested a very large house—probably a mansion. Or maybe we were walking in circles; I would not have known.

A door shut behind us and my hostage-taker said, "We're here."

I pulled off the blindfold and looked around me. I shook my head incredulously. "Is this it?"

"I'm afraid so. We didn't have a choice."

They'd attempted to make the room pleasant for me: there was a real bed with a white lace bedspread, a shaggy rug on the floor, a mini-fridge with a few dishes stacked on top of it, a low bureau with drawers. But it was tiny. If I stretched out my arms, I could almost touch the two side walls, and the open bathroom door reached the foot of the bed. The bathtub he'd promised me was there, cream-colored and shiny, and several folded towels had been piled on a rack above it. Next to the tub lay a basket of bath oils and soaps.

I sat down on the bed. There wasn't even a window in the room. Air came from behind a screen in the ceiling, like in a hotel.

"It's so small," I whined. It was ridiculous—a hostage complaining about accommodations. Even if he loved me, I was still a secret prisoner, not a guest. He had to make sure I wouldn't be found.

"I know this isn't ideal," he said. "But take a look in the top drawer of the bureau."

I reached over and pulled the drawer open.

"A laptop!" I exclaimed, my dismay vanishing in an instant. "Oh, thank you!"

"I'll bring you films to watch," he said. "And I've installed a few games."

I rose from the bed and wrapped my arms around him. "It's all right. I don't mind the room. I guess I won't be going out anymore?"

"I'm sorry. It won't be possible. But I don't think your stay here will be very long. I have to go now but I'll be back tomorrow. There's food in the refrigerator. Any requests?" His voice was cold and formal again, but I knew it was only a front.

"Now that we're in a house, could you make me spaghetti, please?"

"Yes, you can have hot meals now. I won't always be the one bringing your food, though. If you hear three knocks on the door, wait a few minutes before opening it. You'll find a tray on the floor."

"Spooky," I said, almost in a whisper.

He looked at me and I saw something in his eyes I hadn't seen before. He was sad.

"The lock releases automatically if there's a fire," he said.

He opened the door and left. The door locked automatically, too.

Free Chloe

Search this site

home | contact | about us | about Chloe | updates | blog

SEPT 28

Special All-Day Birthday Vigil for Chloe

Please Place Your Own Handmade

FREE CHLOE

Sign in Your Window

CHAPTER 20

As soon as he'd left I filled the tub with hot water, bubble bath, and three bottles of scented oil.

Immersing myself in hot water—as hot as I could stand—was wonderfully soothing after that dark, cramped ride.

I wondered who lived in the house. Did it belong to my hostage-taker? He didn't seem rich, somehow. You could tell, usually, who was well off and who was poor. It must be the woman's house. It was unlikely, now that I thought about it, that she was his mother.

I had sometimes smelled chlorine on him, and I realized now that he must have been swimming here, in an indoor or outdoor pool. I longed to go for a swim too. One day we'd swim together, the two of us. We'd race and dive and twine our bodies underwater.

My imagination wandered to beach vacations and surfing, and I almost fell asleep in the tub. I shook myself awake and grabbed a towel. These towels were softer and larger than the ones in the warehouse. Every small detail became magnified, I realized, when your life was reduced to a single room. You lost perspective, literally.

I examined the contents of the bureau drawers: socks, two tops, a pair of sweatpants, underwear, flannel pajamas, hair-brush, comb, nail file, hand lotion. I tried on the tops. They were a perfect fit: one was a striped green-and-blue tank and the other a long-sleeved pink jersey. I was as happy as a little kid that I had something new to wear. I wondered who had chosen them for me.

The bureau doubled as a night table, and next to the lamp there was a mug with a picture of a shaggy dog on it. I stared at the dog for about ten minutes. "Talk about sensory deprivation," I murmured.

I sat on the bed and checked out the games on the laptop: they were mostly word or puzzle games. There was also a program for learning Italian; it moved me that my hostage-taker had gone to the trouble of finding and installing it, and I felt a wave of affection and gratitude.

I spent the rest of the day playing a game I'd never heard of which was slightly addictive. But despite the distraction of the laptop, I felt almost unbearably caged in. The ceiling seemed to be pressing down on me, and I began to worry about suffocating. What if the vent stopped working?

I considered banging on the door, but I was afraid people in the house who weren't supposed to know about me would hear. I was sure I'd never look at a caged bird the same way again.

I knew I should exercise. I could have run in place, done sit-ups and push-ups, performed a handstand. I could have had a decent workout even in that tiny space, but I wasn't up to it.

Instead I ate a sandwich and got into bed. There was a warm, lightweight quilt under the bedspread and I pulled it up to my ears. *At least I have a comfortable bed with cozy blankets*, I told myself.

When I woke up in the miniscule room I had no idea whether it was six in the morning or six in the evening. I checked the laptop, but for some reason it didn't have the time.

Now I was even more lost than in the warehouse. The watch I had was old and didn't indicate the time of day. Old watch, old mat; private planes, mansions—it confirmed my sense that it was the woman, and not my hostage-taker, who was wealthy.

For breakfast—or was it supper?—I had a banana milk-shake. I looked forward to the pasta dish I'd asked for. That would be the highlight of my day, it seemed.

But I was wrong. When my hostage-taker came to see me he was carrying a bottle of sherry and a vase of purple irises. He handed me the flowers and said, "Many happy returns of the day."

"Oh! Is it my birthday today?" I buried my face in the flowers. The oppression and frustration I'd been feeling began to recede. I was overjoyed to see my hostage-taker, and his gift reminded me that he loved me. *I guess you'd call it love*, he'd said. He was fighting his feelings, but he wouldn't have to fight them if they weren't there in the first place.

"They're celebrating all over your country," he said.

"Don't say 'your country'—it hurts me."

"I only meant the country you live in."

"Is it morning or evening, by the way?"

"Evening. I brought you some films," he said. He emptied two bagfuls of DVDs on the bed.

"Oh, thank you! I can't wait to watch them. Can I have a birthday kiss?"

"I don't think that's a good idea."

But as soon as he sat down on the bed I leaned over and kissed him and, to my delight, he kissed me back. He didn't pull away, he didn't stop himself.

I'd never felt anything so perfect—I didn't know such perfection existed. We'd kissed twice before, but only for a few seconds. This kiss was long and unhurried, and I could tell he wasn't going to pull away. He'd given up trying to resist.

There are a million ways to kiss, as I know from my few experiences and Angie's many reports, and I'd never really enjoyed kissing before. Angie and I had all kinds of funny names for various types of disaster kissing. But this was something altogether different and impossible to describe.

We kissed for a very long time. Every time we paused for breath my hostage-taker said, "This is a huge mistake." But he didn't stop.

For the first time I understood the expression "floating on air"—it was nothing like the experience of hurtling through the air during a floor routine or dismount. That was about focus, control, achievement. You became part of the world, part of its options.

This was about leaving planet Earth altogether.

Finally he said, "Would you care for some sherry?"

"You're so funny," I said. "The way you talk sometimes! So formal."

"Probably because English isn't my first language."

"Or maybe you're just trying to stay detached. I've never met anyone who never smiled. Never ever."

I was surprised by his answer. "I'm sure I smile."

"And you don't say hello or good-bye," I said.

"Don't I?"

"No. And it's quite rude, if you ask me." I was only teasing, of course.

He poured sherry into two glasses and said, "To you."

"Yes, to me," I agreed. "The perfect hostage. And to you, the misguided but well-meaning criminal who is going to see the light and reform."

I sipped the sherry—I'd never actually drunk sherry, and it was better than I'd expected. "What a way to celebrate my eighteenth birthday," I said. "You know, I've never been as scared in my life, and then never as sad, and now I'm the happiest I've ever been."

"That's why I worry, Chloe."

I felt tingly and shivery, hearing him say my name. It was almost as if I had a new name, it sounded so different when he said it.

"I wish I knew your name. Can I make one up?" I asked.

"I don't think that would work."

"I'll just call you sweetie, then."

"I'd rather you didn't."

"You can't control everything … Two control freaks," I laughed. "We're quite the couple!"

"We're not a couple."

"You can be really boring, you know."

"You're falling prey to the Stockholm Syndrome. I'm sure you've heard of it. You imagine you love me, you want to protect me. It feels real, but it's not. You'll see that when you're free."

"You couldn't be more wrong," I said. "I think this hostage-taking idea of yours is completely insane. I don't believe in crime. You can't just take things into your own hands! You can't decide which laws suit you and which ones don't. You could have worked for a retrial without risking your life and terrifying me. If you really love me, why can't you believe that I really love you?"

"You don't know me."

I pulled an iris out of the vase and buried my face in it. The satiny petals tickled my cheek and the delicate, sweet scent was heavenly. If only it could last, that scent ... "Are people really celebrating my birthday?" I asked.

"Yes. It's lucky for us."

"They're turning me into someone I'm not."

"I suppose that's true. But so what? Mythologizing is part of our nature. It doesn't have to be a bad thing."

"Please tell me one thing," I said. "I have to know. How many people know where I am?"

"Two now."

"What if that guy—the addict—told someone before he died?"

"Fortunately, he had no one to tell. He didn't have other people in his life."

"Why take such risks? You can do so much good just by

being a decent person," I said. "You may want to seriously reconsider your lifestyle choices."

"Yes, taking you was risky and dangerous."

"So why do it? Why, why, why?"

"You care more about my life than I do."

My eyes filled with tears. "You're a sad person," I said. "What about the pilot of the plane?" I asked.

"I have a license."

I shuddered. It was impossible not to think of 9/11. He knew that, and he added, "Millions of people know how to pilot a small plane. It takes about three weeks to learn."

"So you're not part of a group?"

"No."

"Who's the woman?"

"She was a friend of my parents'."

"It's frustrating—I want to know everything about you. I can't even place your accent. I know you swim in a swimming pool. And now I know the pool is here, in this house. I like to swim too—I love diving. Do you dive?"

"No."

"I could teach you—it's lots of fun. Oh, I want us to be together always!" I had an image of the two of us in a back-yard, our two little children in a wading pool, our house behind us. We were wearing shorts and throwing a beachball for our kids to catch.

He didn't answer or even look at me. He was staring into space and his face was even more expressionless than usual. He was somewhere else, far away from me.

I waited for him to come back. I heard the faint sound of a car outside, either driving away or arriving.

My hostage-taker broke the silence. "Shall I make the pasta now?"

"Yes, please." I placed my hand on his back, but he immediately removed it.

"Please don't touch me," he said.

"Is that creep Chad still saying he's my boyfriend?" I asked.

"I think he's lost credibility."

"I've never had sex with anyone," I said.

"I know."

"What do you mean?" I asked, confused.

"It's been in the papers."

I felt my cheeks burning. "They're discussing my sexual status in the media?!"

"I told you, you sell many copies of newspapers. They have to think of new things to say."

"Oh, God. I thought high school gossip was bad. Is there anything about me that *hasn't* been discussed?"

"Not much."

"If only I could trust Mom. But she's so naive in some ways."

"She's doing a great job for you, Chloe. She's made the world love you. It's good for us, but it's also good for you."

"What else did they say?"

"Only good things. No one has said anything against you— they'd be stoned alive. You've become everyone's favorite person."

"It's no one's business what I've done and haven't done. I feel I don't have a private life anymore. Whatever, I don't care. What about you? You must have had a lot of girlfriends."

"I've never been with a woman," he replied, looking steadily at me.

"That's impossible!" I said.

"Why?"

"Because of your age—you must be at least twenty-six? And because you're so good-looking—and sexy. Women must have been after you constantly. And besides, how would you know how to kiss like that?"

"It was included in the hostage-taking manual," he said.

I laughed. "So why haven't you dated? Were you in a Buddhist monastery?"

"I was in prison for a long time."

I was shocked when he said that, though I tried not to show it. "Was it for another crazy hostage scheme?"

"It wasn't the sort of place where there had to be a reason."

"Well, what were you accused of?"

"There wasn't any trial. The more I tell you, Chloe, the more complicated it's going to be for you when you come out."

"What does it matter? I'm not going to tell them anything anyhow."

He looked at me as if he was about to hypnotize me. "You have to tell them everything," he said.

"What do you mean?"

"No one will believe I've told you the truth. If you say I mentioned a Catholic community, they'll automatically assume I'm Muslim. If you tell them I said I was in prison, they'll assume I wasn't. So you don't have to worry about that. And don't think for a minute that you can get away with lying. Lying would make things very messy and very horrible for you. It's the worst thing you could possibly do. Instead of being everyone's hero, you'll find yourself in serious trouble. Withholding information that could help them arrest a terrorist, as they see it, will be considered a crime."

"That's crazy. You talk as if I don't have rights."

"Yes, of course you have rights. But you can't imagine you'll get away with lying to professionals. Don't even try, Chloe. They'll know in seconds, and then you'll be in for a very long haul, and an extremely unpleasant one. They'll destroy the image that's been created of you and overnight you'll lose everyone's sympathy."

"I can't reveal everything!" I cried out. "I love my country, but I can't betray you."

"Telling the truth is your only choice and, luckily, it's the best policy. In any case, they'll assume I manipulated everything. They'll assume I sent the other guy to make you vulnerable, and that the story of him dying of an overdose is invented. They'll assume I pretended to know something about medicine, that I left you alone on purpose, that the kids you heard were just taped voices, that the close call on the highway was staged. They'll even assume the broken can opener was part of a strategy."

"And this conversation—do I tell them what you're telling me now?"

"There's no reason not to."

"But ... then they'll know it's a strategy ..."

"No, Chloe. You have to realize that one thing they'll be certain of, no matter what, is that I'm a bad guy. The only reason you don't feel that way yourself is that you've become attached to me. And you've become attached to me because of the situation. That's the only thing you may not want to reveal—your feelings toward me. Because if that leaks to the press it could destroy your life. The people questioning you won't care, but the media would not forgive you. So I'd strongly advise you not to tell anyone, even Angie. The potential harm it could do to you is just not worth it. I'll go make the pasta now. Any special requests?"

"Just come back soon."

Two Convictions on Chloe Mills List Struck Down

The Free Chloe Campaign celebrated a first victory in their efforts to meet the demands of the abductors of Chloe Mills, the U.S. teen who was taken hostage in August this year in Greece.

In two separate reviews, the Fourth Circuit Court of Appeals ruled that evidence had been suppressed in the cases of both Milo Amando and Julian Holmes, and struck down the convictions.

Amando, 46, was serving a life sentence for sedition and conspiracy. Holmes, 38, was serving 25 years for a third-time non-violent felony. The late, controversial Lawrence Mayfair-Horrick prosecuted all the cases on the abductors' list of demands.

The abductors have also requested automatic release for convicted felons Murad Dursun and Samir Basha.

Other demands include parole hearings or transfers for an additional 30 prisoners. Most of the transfers, generally from maximum to minimum security and to prisons closer to home, have been approved, and parole hearings are underway.

"We are in no way, shape or form giving in to terrorists," Secretary of State Lisa Richards said at a press conference today. "Release of prisoners in exchange for hostages has always been and will always be out of the question. The process leading to review and transfers was instigated by concerned citizens, and that is their right. Decisions were made entirely within the bounds of our legal system—a system which these events have proved once again to be among the best in the world."

POST REPORT

CHAPTER 21

As soon as he'd left I spread the DVDs on the bed.

There were twenty-six movies in all. They were all in English and they were all old. I recognized some of the actors' names—Doris Day, for example—but apart from one or two famous titles, I'd never heard of any of them.

I chose *Pillow Talk* at random, or maybe because it rang a vague bell. I slid it into the drive and began to watch.

A strange thing happened then. Everything in the movie—every scene, every word, even the credits—excited me. I was thrilled by the tacky furniture, the old cars, the view of a bridge through the window. It was almost as if the characters were keeping me company.

I had no idea how I'd relate to the movie in ordinary circumstances. I just couldn't tell. I didn't know whether I'd normally consider the jokes lame, whether I'd consider the whole movie lame. As far as I was concerned, *Pillow Talk* was the greatest film ever made.

The only thing I was still able to judge was the annoying soundtrack and the way people related to sex, which was sometimes odd.

It was the same with all the films. I liked the over-the-top way the women talked in the dramas, I liked their semi-fake accents. Most of the movies were in black and white; I was amazed by how many shades of grey there were. I was aware that the stories were repetitive and meandering, but I didn't mind because every scene was mesmerizing. I enjoyed the drawn-out plots; I enjoyed drifting along with them.

I remember all the movies vividly—partly because I saw most of them two or three or even four times, and partly because the experience was so intense. I saw *The Philadelphia Story, I'll See You in My Dreams, An American in Paris, The Children's Hour, Gaslight, All About Eve, East of Eden,* and a dozen others. My sleep was filled with fragmented scenes from the day's viewings. In some of the dreams I was in the scenes, trying to fit in. It seemed urgent not to let anyone know I was from the future, and I tried frantically to find hats with feathers and old-style clothes so no one would notice.

I didn't see my hostage-taker for over a week. My meals were brought to me by the invisible person who knocked three times and quickly left.

The food was more conventional now: scrambled eggs or porridge for breakfast; soup, salad, and a cheese sandwich for lunch; lasagna or quiche for supper. Chocolate milk or milk-shake twice a day. And for dessert, ice cream, vanilla pudding, cake. Sometimes I left notes on the tray when I sent it back. *Thanks for the salad but could you please put less salt in the dressing?* Or, *I wouldn't mind pizza, no anchovies.*

I was on the bed, lying on my stomach and watching *Christmas in Connecticut,* when my hostage-taker returned. He was carrying a tray with a ceramic serving dish and a large bowl of salad.

I was so desperate for company I didn't even try to hold back. As soon as he set down the tray, I jumped into his arms and wrapped my legs around him. He was wearing his black jeans but he had on a plaid button-up instead of his usual white shirt. It was a treat, seeing him in a casual top; he was letting me glimpse another side of his life. I felt madly attracted to him.

He tried to lower me onto the bed, but I wouldn't let go. I brought him down with me. "You're trapped now," I said. "Trapped with me. I won't let you leave."

"Our meal will get cold," he said, gently releasing himself from my grasp.

"How long are you staying?" I asked.

"I don't have to be anywhere else today."

"Please stay the night. I can't bear the loneliness in this room."

"We'll talk about it later."

"What's for supper?"

"Fettuccini with cream sauce."

"Alfredo?" I asked.

"Something like that."

As we ate I told him about the movies I'd seen. "How come they're all oldies?" I asked.

"I'm afraid that's all I could get. I was hoping at least some would be to your liking."

"I love them."

"I'm glad."

Dessert was chocolate ice cream. "My consolation prize," I said. "For being stuck here. What's happened to my books, by the way?"

"I haven't had a chance to pick them up," he said.

"Could I have a notebook and pen at least? It's not the

same, typing onscreen … Will you stay the night?" I asked again.

"I don't think that's a good idea. Look what happened last time." He meant the time he held me in his sleep.

"Nothing happened last time," I reminded him. "Please stay. I can tell you want to."

"What I want isn't important."

"And what about what I want? Doesn't that count at all?"

"Yes, it counts."

"Will you at least stay to watch a movie with me? A movie date …"

He considered for a few seconds. Then he said, "All right, I'll stay the night, Chloe. But there have to be some ground rules."

I laughed. "You're a lot like me, you know. Everything has to be planned in advance. That's a good thing, that we're alike. It means we understand each other. Okay, what are the rules?"

"I know we might end up kissing again. We've crossed that line once and that makes it hard to resist a second time, both for you and for me. But I don't want you touching me."

"Okay," I said, switching off the lamp. The room was thrown into darkness; the only source of light was the glare of the screen.

"It's not about boundaries," he said, his face shadowy in the dim light. "It's a personal request."

I felt better when he said that. "Can we watch a movie together?"

"Yes. But you must keep your promise."

"You can tie my hands behind my back again to make sure."

"Don't joke about such things," he said.

www.free-chloe.org

Free Chloe

Search this site

home | contact | about us | about Chloe | updates | blog

Dear friends and supporters,

Thank you for everything you've been doing to help Chloe. We're really happy with the outcomes of the first two trials.

There has been much speculation about the recent silence from the people holding Chloe.

Please let's not imagine the worst. We don't even know whether they really are being silent or whether we are simply not being told about their latest communications.

Please be patient and remain hopeful.

Love,

Allegra

CHAPTER 22

Watching a movie on the laptop turned out to be impossible unless we were in the same line of vision. I ended up lying against him, with my head on his chest and his arm around my shoulder. He stroked my arm almost absently as the movie began. It was thrilling, that simple gesture of affection.

I'd chosen *It Happened One Night* because it was light and also because it was about a couple who were thrown together by chance. But I could tell he wasn't concentrating. Before long we were kissing again.

I wanted more than kissing, but I knew it was out of the question for him. He did something better. He said, "My father was a great Chaplin fan."

He was bringing down the barrier, if only for a moment. I seized on it. "Is he still alive?"

"No, both my parents died when I was young."

"How?" I asked, though I didn't expect an answer. I assumed he'd shut down on me any minute.

But he replied, in his usual casual way, "They were killed by the regime."

"The regime? What do you mean?"

"They spoke out against the dictatorship and paid the price."

"How horrible!"

"I had a pet tortoise, and on the day my father was arrested I was in the garden reading a book of stories, and I allowed my tortoise to walk on the pages, which I knew

I wasn't supposed to do, because it was my father's book, a very nice edition. And my father came into the garden to say good-bye. I think he knew that was the end for him, and that this was a final good-bye. I don't know how he controlled himself, but he did. I quickly took the tortoise off the page, but he saw that the page was wet, and I was so ashamed that I didn't answer when he said good-bye. When I realized a few days later that he wasn't coming back I felt so guilty and miserable I made a small bonfire in the garden and I burned the book."

"I'm so sorry!" I exclaimed, though I kept my voice low, barely above a whisper. I didn't want to break the spell of intimacy. "How old were you?"

"I was fourteen when my father was arrested. My mother managed to hold on one more year, then she vanished."

"I don't understand. You mean she might be alive?"

"No, they were both killed. But I'll never know where or how."

"There wasn't any sort of … record, or something?"

"No. One day they were there and the next they were gone. All I can hope is that it was fast, though I know the odds are against it."

"That's so sad."

"You lost a parent too, so you know what it's like."

"I was very young, and besides, it wasn't both my parents, and they weren't just … killed." Tears welled up in my eyes. "Some stories are too sad to bear."

"But have you noticed only other people's stories? Because ours are just the things that happen to us."

I shook my head. "No, I don't agree. I think sometimes our own stories are also too sad to bear. That's why people die of grief."

"I need some coffee, Chloe," he said. "I'll be right back. Would you like something?"

"More ice cream, please."

"I'm sorry about the locked door—it locks automatically. I'll only be a few minutes."

I felt happy and heartbroken at the same time. Happy because he'd trusted me and we were closer now—there was no going back. And heartbroken because of what he'd told me. I wondered what country it had happened in. Unfortunately, there were probably several that fit the description.

He returned a few minutes later with ice cream and coffee. He'd reverted to the casual formality that made him seem detached and remote. When he sat down, he held the coffee mug as if it was a barrier between him and the world.

"How come you were never worried about me seeing you?" I asked, hoping to draw him back to me.

"Even Rembrandt only captured one expression from one angle. Anyhow, I'm not the sort of person anyone would suspect."

"What about your prison record?"

"I don't have one. One good thing about that prison, the only good thing, is that there are no records. People came in, died or didn't die, were executed or not executed, left or didn't leave. No one knows who was in and who wasn't."

"And you complain about the U.S."

"I don't remember making any complaints."

"I just assumed ..."

"There's injustice everywhere. No one is exempt. It's human nature, apparently."

We were quiet for a while. I thought about what he'd told me, and suddenly a piece of the puzzle seemed to fall into place. "Is that where you met the prisoner you're trying to help?" I asked. "In that prison?"

"Yes. He's older than me, and he saved my life. I owe him this."

"How did he end up in jail again?"

"Some old enemy seeking revenge, pointing a finger at him, accusing him of planning a terrorist act. With all the paranoia these days he didn't stand a chance. And he was given life in maximum security, without any evidence other than his enemy's statements and some meaningless things he had written on scraps of paper found on his desk."

"What bad luck, to be arrested twice ... but what if they try to locate everyone who ever knew the prisoner you're trying to get released? What if they make a list of all his friends?"

"Luckily I'm not on that list."

"Someone from that prison might remember you as his friend."

"We were all just trying to stay alive. No one was interested in anyone else's name or identity. The less we all knew, the better for our survival, emotionally and otherwise. Unfortunately, almost everyone who was in there with me is probably dead by now."

"I know I shouldn't be prying."

"That word, prying, reminds me of something. In prison there was a man with an incredible sense of humor. If the food was particularly inedible, he would lean over and say in English, *Would I be prying if I asked you whether you detected a hint of tarragon in the soup?* I think of him always when I make food."

"Did he make it?"

He stared down into his coffee, and his pain showed in the way his hands held the mug. "No, he died before I left."

"Was he executed?"

"He came down with a fever and died in the infirmary."

"They had an infirmary in a place like that?"

"Even Nazi camps had infirmaries. It creates an illusion of normalcy, which for some reason the people in charge need to maintain. It's just another form of torture, pretending there's any sort of caring going on. Or maybe it's just to prevent an epidemic that would kill everyone off and also jeopardize the guards."

"I feel so sad and I didn't even know him."

"Yes, he was a wonderful fellow."

"Thank you for trusting me. I won't say anything to anyone, ever."

"I told you—no matter what you report, they'll assume that everything I'm telling you is a lie. In fact, the best thing I could do for my case is—" He stopped in his tracks. It was the first time he hadn't thought through what he was going to say, and he looked confused and a little embarrassed. I was very moved, seeing those emotions on his face.

"Is what?" I urged.

He said, in his most I'm-in-control voice, "The best thing for me would be to have sex with you, that would absolutely settle it, for them."

I laughed. "We're in a looking-glass world. Everything's inside out ... What if they think I'm making everything up, even if I tell the truth?"

"That won't happen. They're trained in interrogation and you're not. That's why telling the truth is the best and easiest thing you can do. If they pick up that you identified with me, they'll blame the Stockholm Syndrome. It won't be in their interest to let that leak. At least I hope that's the case."

"You still think that's what I have—the Stockholm Syndrome?"

"Yes."

"That means you don't really love me either?"

"No, that part is real. I never thought I'd fall in love, after all I've been through. But yes, I've fallen in love with you."

It took all the control I had not to hoot. Instead I said calmly, "Doesn't that mean you want us to be together?"

"Yes, in theory. But it's just not possible."

"I don't accept that. Why not apply to university? We could go to the same one and meet that way. Your rich friend can afford it, I'm assuming."

"It's not a question of cost."

"What would your mother want for you? A life of crime and danger, or a career and family?" I regretted the question as soon as I asked it, and I covered my mouth in dismay. He'd trusted me with his tragic story, and I was already using it against him, to score a point. "I'm sorry, I'm sorry," I said.

"This is a situation where you don't need to apologize for anything, Chloe. My mother would want me to go to university and have a family, of course."

"Then please, please promise never to do anything like this again!"

"How can I make any promises about the future? How can anyone?"

"Of course people can! When it comes to morals and values you have to be able to promise. It's a promise you make to yourself—not to lie, not to steal, to be a good person."

"Yes, that's true."

"Being a good person includes not taking the law into your own hands."

"There would never have been a legal review if not for this abduction and all the pressure it created."

"Even if that's true—even if it worked once, it doesn't mean it was the right thing to do. It definitely doesn't mean it will work a second time. And you'll never know, will you, whether you'd have managed to get what you wanted in some other way."

"In theory."

"Well, theory is everything. Action has to be based on theory, not on wild impulse."

"They said in the newspaper you were smart."

"Everyone's smart in some ways, dumb in others. That's what Angie always says. Look at you. You're smart, but this hostage idea is beyond dumb. That man—the addict. Was he your brother?"

My hostage-taker was very startled. He tried not to show it, but he was completely taken aback. I knew from his reaction that my guess was right, and he knew that I knew.

I said, "Something about the way you talked about him ... something made me think, on the way here, that he was your brother."

"It's because I'm the only person you see that you become hypersensitive to everything I say and the way I say it," he said, avoiding the question.

"Let's not talk anymore. You'll stay the night like you promised?"

"Did I promise?"

"Yes."

"How about I stay until you fall asleep?"

"I'll take what I can get."

Kimmy Xuan good morning hun! I know you weren't happy with the whole Win A Date With Chloe idea, but I watched it of course along with everyone else (ratings through the roof apparently) and it really wasn't bad. The guys were really cool and they ALL talked about the campaign. And that dude from NBA—wow! In the end it was harmless fun and a good way of keeping her in the news which is what we're trying to do, no?

15 minutes ago   Comment   Like   Wall-to-wall

Angie Shaw Thanks, Kimmy for being so positive. It's just that all the laughing and joking seems wrong when it's possible that Chloe is being raped and tortured. But I'm being hypersensitive I know. The counselor at school keeps reminding us that the best thing we can do for Chloe is keep our spirits up. Chloe might be very excited about dating at least one of those guys esp with that cruise package. But everything depends on what shape she's in when she gets back.

11 minutes ago   Comment   Like   Wall-to-wall

Jeanette Persky She's coming back to hot dates and a LOT of money for selling her story. I think that can make up for whatever she went through.

8 minutes ago   Comment   Like   Wall-to-wall

Angie Shaw I can't believe you said that. Read Telling by Patricia Weaver. If Chloe's going through hell she might NEVER recover, or it could take years and years. Sorry if I'm coming across too strong.

6 minutes ago   Comment   Like   Wall-to-wall

Jeanette Persky yeah you completely misunderstood I was trying to do what you were saying which is be upbeat but I guess it's impossible to talk to you these days.

3 minutes ago   Comment   Like   Wall-to-wall

Angie Shaw sorry sorry sorry. yes I misunderstood. Didn't mean to go all crazy on you. Come to the meeting tonight, my place at 7, my mom's making enchiladas. luv u

1 minute ago   Comment   Like   Wall-to-wall

CHAPTER 23

The terrifying sound of machine-gun fire woke me up. I knew instantly what the sound was—I had no doubt at all. I reached out frantically for my hostage-taker, but he wasn't there. He'd left while I was sleeping.

I didn't know what to think—panic had frozen not only my body but also my brain. Was it the police, had they found out about me? Would they come tearing down to the basement looking for me?

Or were these friends of the addict? Were they here to take revenge?

I grabbed the quilt, wrapped it around myself, and rolled under the bed. My heart was beating so hard I was sure anyone who came into the room would hear it, and I was shaking, or rather shuddering, from head to toe.

There was another burst of gunfire, though it seemed more distant now—maybe the gunmen were on the upper floor of the house.

And then it was quiet. The quiet seemed eerie. No footsteps, no one leaving, no cars driving away. What if everyone in the house was dead?

I stayed under the bed for a long time. The panic receded as the minutes ticked by—the longer I waited, the less likely it was that they'd come downstairs looking for me. I was very confused—I didn't know what to do, what to think.

I must have dozed off eventually, cocooned inside the soft quilt, because I dreamed I came out of my room and began creeping slowly upstairs when suddenly I saw a severed hand on the stairs. I knew I mustn't scream; instead I forced myself to wake up.

After what seemed like an eternity there was a knock on the door and I heard my hostage-taker's voice saying, "Chloe?"

I scrambled out from under the bed. "You're alive!" I cried out.

"Yes, were you worried?"

"Well, of course I was worried! What happened? I was hiding under the bed all night."

"Why were you hiding?"

"The shooting, of course!"

"Chloe, there hasn't been any shooting. You must have had a bad dream."

"I didn't dream it—I heard it. Machine-gun fire and heavy footsteps."

"There wasn't anything like that."

"Where were you?" I asked frantically. I couldn't have dreamed it—it was impossible. He must have been away and didn't know what had happened in his absence.

"I've been upstairs the entire time. No one's been here."

"What time is it?"

"8:15."

I sat down on the bed and tried to gather my thoughts. Maybe being enclosed in such a small room was making me hallucinate. But it had seemed so real. I began to cry with confusion, frustration, relief.

"I'm going to take a bath," I said, wiping away tears. "If I draw the curtain can I keep the door open? I want to make sure you don't leave."

"I won't leave. I have the day off today."

I ran a bath with the scented oils and bubble foam. "I must be losing my mind," I said from behind the curtain. "Literally. I heard machine-gun fire. Twice. The first time was really close, the second time was more distant. I didn't know what to think."

"You just had a vivid dream, Chloe," he said. "You're under a lot of stress."

"Nothing like a hot bath," I sighed, shutting my eyes. "I used to soak for hours when I was training …"

"Do you mind if I smoke?"

"Of course I mind! In case you haven't noticed, this place is about the size of a hamster cage … I didn't know you smoked." I peeked out from the edge of the curtain. He was sitting on the floor, facing the side wall. He was as still as a statue—a classical statue of Apollo, or maybe some emperor, seen in profile. His arm was resting on his raised knee and he was holding a pack of cigarettes in his hand. I couldn't see the brand.

"I don't usually," he said, without turning his head. "Smoking reminds me of prison, in fact. But I found a pack lying around in the kitchen, and I'm suddenly in the mood."

"Why does it remind you of prison?"

"The guards smoked."

"That reminds me—I keep meaning to ask you, how come you gave me mouth-to-mouth? Isn't that for when people drown?"

He continued to stare at the wall. "I couldn't think of anything else."

"Do you work in a hospital?"

"Not exactly."

"I guess you saved my life."

"I endangered your life."

"You like anatomy and all that stuff, I can tell."

He paused, then said, "My father was a physician. I began studying medicine too, but I was arrested before I got very far."

"Do you live here? In this house?"

"No."

"Does the woman?"

"Don't ask so many questions, Chloe."

"I'm coming out. I guess I'm feeling better. Will you stay? We can watch another movie."

I grabbed a towel and stepped out of the bath. I didn't feel like getting dressed right away. Instead, I lay on the bed with the towel wrapped around me.

"I'm desperate for a massage," I said.

I didn't think my more-than-obvious ploy would work, but to my surprise he said, "If you get dressed I'll give it a go."

I pulled on the sweats and a T-shirt and lay on my stomach. He kneeled next to me on the bed and slid his hands under my T-shirt. For a few seconds his hands lay motionless on my back, as if I were a specimen from outer space that he was curious about. Then slowly he began locating different muscles. I never imagined I could derive so much pleasure from mere touch. I felt myself falling into a semi-trance; at the same time it was as if I was discovering my own body. A body that had once been my obsession as I worked for hours each day, trying to make it stretch and spin and land in precise ways. But this was different. It was an exploration, not just for him, but for me too.

When he finished, he lay down next to me and we held each other in silence. I forgot about the no-touching rule, or maybe now that we were so close I assumed it didn't apply any longer. I reached out and touched his cheek.

It was a small, spontaneous gesture, but his response was almost violent. He pushed my hand away forcefully and sat up. He seemed to be under immense strain. "I asked you not to do that," he said angrily.

I had no idea what was going on. He wasn't struggling with desire—it wasn't that at all. Something about my gesture had upset him. Something that had nothing to do with me.

"I'm sorry," I said. "I forgot."

He shook his head, no longer angry. "No, it's I who should apologize. I had some memories intruding."

"Is it from your time in jail? Did the other prisoners … you know—try things with you?" I knew I shouldn't be asking, but I couldn't help myself.

"No," he said. "It wasn't that sort of prison. We were barely even able to talk to one another. We sat in a large cell and we were more or less watched all the time. You had to bribe the guard just so he wouldn't punish you for whispering."

"Tell me what it was like for you there."

"I don't want to talk about my time in prison, Chloe. It would upset you, and there's no point."

"But I'd like to know. It's an important part of your life."

"I'm not sure I'm up to it. I don't want to go back there, even in conversation."

"You can give me a shortened version."

"I wouldn't even know where to start."

"Tell me what an average day was like." It wasn't only that I wanted to know. I felt he was carrying the weight of his experiences, and that it would be better for him if he talked about them.

He paused, trying to decide whether to continue.

After a long silence, he said, "The biggest problem in the beginning was fear. When you first arrive, they're after you a lot. But then they get bored, or maybe when you get weaker they want to move on to someone who will respond more. After a while I was only called every few weeks, mostly because some influential friends on the outside were paying bribes. Three entire years I was forgotten altogether, and I was beginning to think that it was permanent. But then out of the blue I was relocated. Relocation is always dreaded—because almost always it's for the worse. And there was one guard everyone feared. It was said that no one survived once they'd been put in his charge."

His face was different as he spoke. He didn't look impassive now. He looked like someone in an old painting, one of those classical paintings with men in robes looking puzzled.

"What do you mean, called? You mean for interrogation?"

"Yes, in theory. Interrogation under torture. But my

friend—the one who's the reason you're here—he helped me with that as soon as I arrived. He told me that at first it might seem there are no boundaries, but that in fact there were boundaries and that I didn't have to fear the unknown. He told me exactly what to expect. Even if they threaten, they won't go past a certain point."

He paused, then went on. "You have to think of it as intimidation. It's true that you're too disgusted to admit to things you haven't done. It's preferable to die. Death at least puts an end to pain. That's why sometimes they torture your family members instead. I can't think of anything worse, but I was spared that particular nightmare. What my friend explained to me is that there isn't anything you can say to make them stop. First, you haven't got any information. It's just a way to increase the prison population, by being able to say, well, such and such a person, while only half alive by the way, said you were subversive. If you admitted you despised the regime, you had to give the names of all your friends. If on the other hand you lied and said you were loyal and obedient, they wanted proof in the form of a name. And then if you gave a name, it meant you were guilty, because you had that knowledge, and it meant you had more names and probably also that you should in fact be executed. The paranoia and ignorance—it was beyond anything. On the other hand, you could be released suddenly, if someone with money or influence was making an effort on your behalf. It was Kafka territory. Or maybe Swift."

I was having difficulty grasping everything he was saying.

"What about that guard?" I asked.

"Yes, the guard. I don't know what happened, something slipped in the system. Bribes were coming in on my behalf, and I wasn't supposed to end up with him. But either he got his eye on me or a bribe got stolen in transit. I was taken through a tunnel to an underground cell. There was almost no air, and I was on my own, and I had one arm and one leg chained. The heat in that cell was indescribable, the light was on all the time, and I can't begin to describe the dirt and stench. It's strange, but the body goes into different gear, a hyper-protective mode, and things that ordinarily would kill you, don't. It would be very interesting to study that phenomenon and see how it works—we could make good use of it if we understood it better.

"Well, I wanted to die and I tried to die, but my body refused. And then after a week or two I got lucky, as I saw it then. I got septicemia, which is fatal without treatment, sometimes even with treatment. I was relieved that the suffering would be over and I was finally going to die.

"But the man who'd helped me was working on my behalf. He managed to bribe a guard to contact my friends outside and let them know I was in danger—because everyone in the prison knew about this guard. My friends began frantic efforts on my behalf, and the day I diagnosed myself, I was pulled out of my cell. I was sure they were taking me for execution and I was glad. But I found myself in the back seat of a car with my two friends. I was sure I was hallucinating. They began to protest that they were given the wrong prisoner because they didn't recognize me at first. I had a beard by then, and I was probably only hours away from giving up the ghost.

"Anyway I pulled through, thanks to that man. I owe him my life."

We sat in silence for a while. I didn't trust myself to talk, and I also felt he didn't want me to say anything. I knew that what he most wanted was for me to relate to him in exactly the same way as before. When he told me about these things, he was trusting me not to change the way I felt about him, not to see him differently. I would have to force myself to be as casual as he was.

But I had goose bumps, and I was in pain. For him it was in the past, but for me it was in the present, and I was filled with grief.

The silence became oppressive; it was separating us from each other. I had to find a way back to him. I asked, "How did you survive five years in a place like that? Psychologically, I mean."

"Well, I didn't entirely. I lost myself for a while."

"Lost yourself?"

He got up, used the toilet, and came back to the room. He leaned against the bureau and gazed down at me. He looked almost amused. "Yes. I had strange habits for the first year. I couldn't bear for anyone to touch me, not even to shake my hand. In the hospital I took my own blood pressure, gave myself injections when possible, I even tried to put in my own IV. When someone touched me I jumped. I think it was partly neurological, some neural damage probably, and it takes a while for the nervous system to repair itself. The rest was really neurotic. I would only eat food I made myself—I couldn't eat at restaurants or other people's houses. Eating meat was out of the question, I couldn't even watch other people eat meat, it seemed to me they were eating human flesh. I could no longer stand up to urinate, I had to sit, otherwise I'd feel faint. I read books backwards, starting at the last page and moving back page by page. Sometimes I couldn't see, everything went black. Nights were hard, I had enormous guilt about my friends who were still in prison. So I spent my nights just walking through London—that's where I was at the time. I felt like Dracula, haunting the dark streets before getting back into my coffin. Weirdest of all, I identified with objects. I projected feelings onto them. If I saw a cup with a broken handle I felt bad for that cup."

"I can hardly bear to think of you in that state," I said.

"It's interesting—physical pain can be forgotten. No matter how terrible it is, how helpless you were, you recover. Your body repairs itself, and though you might be depressed afterwards, you don't really remember the pain. But sexual degradation is completely different. It haunts you, it just won't let go. No matter how hard you try to get rid of it, you can't. And it's the hardest thing to talk about, too."

"I'm sorry I was so insensitive."

"How could you have known? Anyway, that's the last word I'd use about you."

"But rationally you know you weren't degraded," I said. "That guard degraded himself. You managed to survive, but he's not even human."

"He's very human, that's the problem. It's as if there was a camera there and the whole world saw me. It's as if everyone can still see it. Rationally I know that's not the case, but I haven't succeeded in convincing myself emotionally."

"Mr. Hostage-Taker?"

"Yes."

"You're still lost."

Two More Reversals for Chloe Mills

Campaign Organizers Celebrate as Another Two Convicts on Demand List Are Exonerated

CHAPTER 24

For a while—I don't know exactly how long—I was all right. I exercised until I was on the verge of collapse; it was the only way I could deal with the confined space. I ran in place, I did four hundred jumping jacks, I got through as many push-ups and sit-ups as possible. I soaked in the bath, played video games, watched movies.

My hostage-taker usually came to see me in the evenings, after I'd eaten. His visits kept me sane. His visits and my love for him.

My breakdown happened suddenly.

We were eating an Indian curry and watching *Brief Encounter* when suddenly, out of the blue, I lost it. I don't know why. Maybe it was the room—being cooped up in that tiny place without even a window to let me know if it was day or night. Even in solitary confinement, prisoners are probably allowed into a courtyard once a day.

Or maybe it was the barriers my hostage-taker kept putting up between us—he never let things progress beyond kissing, and he never allowed me to touch him.

And he didn't talk about himself again. He listened when I described my school, my friends, things that had happened to me. But he said nothing more about his past, and we didn't discuss our feelings for each other. I began to feel that he was kissing me as a kind of favor, out of a sense of obligation, because he knew I needed it and didn't have the heart to refuse.

Or maybe my breakdown had to do with what my

hostage-taker had been through in prison. It took a few days for what he'd told me to really sink in, and then the images he'd conjured began to haunt me. At night when I shut my eyes I saw him chained up in a filthy cell with that monster, or sitting with all the other prisoners, waiting to be called.

What did they actually do to him? I didn't dare ask—I wasn't sure I could bear to know. I wondered whether he wore long sleeves because he had scars on his arms.

Whatever the reason, I suddenly jumped out of his arms, swiped the laptop to the floor, and began throwing myself against the walls. I was weeping and thrashing and screaming hysterically. I had to get out of that room. It was a physical need. I felt I would die if I had to stay in there one more minute.

My hostage-taker tried to hold me, but I escaped from his arms. I wasn't myself; I was like someone possessed. "Let me out, let me out!" I shouted. I would have run out the door, but he was standing in front of it.

At last I calmed down enough for him to speak. He said, "If you give me a few minutes, Chloe, you can step out."

I nodded. I couldn't have spoken even if I'd wanted to; uncontrollable gasps and sobs were half choking me.

He went out. I heard furniture being moved, footsteps retreating, returning, more sounds of things being moved. I curled up in a fetal position on the floor, moaning. My hostage-taker came over and said, "You can come out now, Chloe." He didn't say it in his usual detached way. His voice was soft, almost inaudible.

I stepped into a larger space, about the size of a billiard room. White sheets had been draped over the furniture. There was nothing to see, nowhere to go. It was a larger room and better than nothing, but it was empty, windowless, and bare.

I lay flat on my back on the polished hardwood floor, exhausted and ashamed. I stretched my arms sideways and muttered, "I'm just a drama queen."

He lay down next to me on the floor, placed his hand on my belly. I pulled his hand to my breasts; I felt almost faint with longing and love. I felt at that moment that I would have done anything at all for him—I would have given my life if I had to.

He said, "Wait," and left me there, lying on the floor, dazed and emptied out.

When he came back he shut off all the lights. Though I could hardly believe it was happening, we both undressed. I hoped he would not see the tears of emotion—a whole universe of swirling emotions—welling in my eyes.

CHAPTER 25

"Do you believe in fate?" I asked. "Our meeting seems so wild, so unlikely. But now that we've met, it's as if it had to happen."

We were sitting on the polished wood floor, eating potato chips from a large bowl. He'd dressed in the dark and gone to get the chips while I bathed. I felt pure and clean and happy.

"One could probably define all of human history as a series of wild and unlikely events," he said.

"You know, you're a very pessimistic person, in some ways. I mean, I guess taking a hostage in the hope of getting a superpower to release some prisoner is a pretty optimistic thing to do. Or maybe that's just recklessness, not optimism."

"I believe there are good people in the world," he said. "I suppose a pessimist would not see that, or would not care."

"Listen. We need to plan how we're going to meet in the future. We can set a time and a place—the Met, for example, in New York. In the Rodin room."

"You can't seriously think you'd get away with such a scheme, Chloe. I'd be an immediate suspect."

"You told me you weren't the sort of person anyone would suspect."

"I was referring to the people who know me."

"There has to be a way," I insisted.

"I can't think of one."

"But they'd have to prove that you were my hostage-taker. Suspicion is one thing, but if we get married and you're a citizen, that's that. People can gossip and guess all they want."

"It isn't so simple, Chloe. You'd never be able to carry it off. Nor should you. You can't live your entire life in a lie."

"Would you marry me if you could?"

"Chloe, you're going home tomorrow."

Tomorrow! I couldn't believe it. "Was your demand met?" I asked, my shaky voice betraying me.

"Yes."

The thought of seeing Mom and my friends, the thought of being safe at home, of being free to go wherever I wanted— it seemed almost surreal, as if my past was some sort of dream-world that no longer existed.

I shook my head. We had to come up with a plan first. I couldn't bear leaving him without something to hold on to.

"We have to have a plan, something," I said, almost in tears.

"There isn't time. The longer you stay here, the more dangerous it is for me."

I knew he was right. Leaving right away was the best thing I could do for him, for us. But I couldn't accept that we were parting forever.

I said, "What about the woman, your parents' friend? Maybe she can say she's a journalist. She can come to the States to interview me. And you could be her photographer. No one would suspect anything, especially after a few months have passed."

"In a few months your feelings will be completely different, Chloe. You'll wonder how you could have been so deluded."

"You're so completely wrong," I said. "But I understand

now. It's because of everything that happened to you … Don't you see that I'll think of nothing but you?"

I paused; an idea had come to me. I said, "I'm going to have a code, so I can send you messages. Every time you read or see in an interview 'There's nothing like the sun rising over the Aegean,' it will mean *I love you.*"

"All right."

"I never thought it was possible to love someone this much."

"Chloe, I don't want to hurt you, but I have to say this. If your feelings change, you may want to cooperate with the authorities. If we planned to meet, I'd have no way of knowing whether it was a trap."

He was right—I was hurt. Hurt and shocked.

"How could you think that! Even if I didn't love you—which will never happen—do you think I want you to spend the rest of your days in San Quentin or maybe even be executed? How can you think I'm that kind of person? You've done time already, for no crime at all. Why would I want you to suffer again?"

"I don't think we can decide anything now, Chloe. And in the meantime we have to talk about logistics."

I sighed. There was nothing more I could say. He didn't trust me because he couldn't see into my soul. Whether we met again was now in his hands, and in the hands of fate. It would have terrified me to think that he might be slipping away from me forever, but I refused to believe it.

"Tomorrow, after dark, I'll give you a disguise—you'll

bathe, trim your nails, and then put on the clothes and the wig. I'll lead you to a car. You'll be taken to a plane and then to another car. I'll give you something to make you sleepy."

"Same stuff as last time?"

"Yes. We'll wake you when we've arrived in Greece. You'll be in a parked car near the Holiday Inn in Athens. Get out of the car—there will be a bench there in case you need to sit. When you're ready, go into the hotel and take the elevator to room 2111. You'll find a key to the door in your purse. Go in and lock the door behind you. There will be more clothes to change into, including a red baseball cap. Take off the old things, put them in the empty plastic bag you'll find on the bed, and leave them outside the door at 4:00 p.m. Can you remember that?"

"Four o'clock. Bag outside door."

"Before putting on the new clothes take a shower and shampoo, then a bath, then another shower. You've got to scrub really well. After that it's up to you. You can stay in the room as long as you like—we've paid for two days, including meals—just use room service. Whatever you do, don't make any outside calls. Not from the room, not from the lobby, not from a store, not from a borrowed cell phone. And no Internet either, even if it's an Internet café or someone's borrowed device. Can you promise?"

I nodded.

"When you feel you can't wait any longer, leave the hotel, walk for at least three blocks, and hail a taxi. Don't talk to anyone, no matter what. Take the taxi to the United States

Embassy. Lose the hat and sunglasses as you step into the taxi. Just let them fall on the curb. No one will notice. Try not to mention the hotel until a few days have passed."

"Wait. What if I'm stopped at the door of the Holiday Inn?"

"Just show them your key. But no one will stop you. It's a busy hotel. And you'll be well dressed. When you get to the embassy, ask for a bathroom with a shower. In the hullabaloo, they won't think twice."

"Hullabaloo?" I smiled in spite of everything.

"Is that the wrong word?"

"No, no," I said. "It's just funny."

"That will be your last chance to wash. Same routine— shower and shampoo."

"On TV they find DNA no matter how hard the criminals try to conceal it."

"Luckily for us, it isn't that simple."

"What do I tell them about my release?"

"Tell the truth, but try to delay the debriefing as long as you can. Say you're not up to it. When you tell them, you can say you cooperated out of fear. It's the only lie you'll have to tell, and even if they see through it, I very much doubt they'll hold it against you."

"What if I hadn't fallen in love with you? How would you have dealt with my release?"

"We would have managed. I apologize for everything, Chloe. I regret putting you through so much."

"It was worth it for me. I wouldn't have met you otherwise."

"You'll be in my thoughts always."

"Don't say that! We're going to meet again, I know it. And if you take another female hostage I'll kill you!" I said.

He tilted his head. "I promise that won't happen."

Then he smiled.

CHAPTER 26

I don't want to think about my last day—it makes me too sad. My hostage-taker stayed with me until it was time to go; he only left to make coffee and bring down food, but neither of us could eat. I took his hand and held it to my cheek, trying to imprint it on my skin.

I felt like a condemned person, with the minutes ticking away. Condemned to part from my true love, as if he were going off to war. I wanted time to stand still, I wanted to find a way to hold on to him forever.

But he had broken the law, and there was no going back on that. Breaking the law is a final act, an act that can't be reversed. He'd have to hide that part of his life always, and if we met again I'd have to hide it too. You couldn't erase a crime, but unless you did something really drastic, you could make up for it by doing good.

When the time came to go, I was in a hyper state of nerves that luckily took up all the available space in my mind. Now I knew what spies felt like. There was nothing else in the world, there was only you and your task.

I was surprised by my pre-performance butterflies. Even at gym meets, I didn't suffer all that much from stage fright and nerves. I liked it when my turn came.

But I was suddenly very nervous and scared. What if I did something wrong? What if we were caught? There were so many parts to the journey—anything could happen. What if I made some horrible mistake and it was my fault that my hostage-taker was caught?

But everything went as planned. I washed and put on an outfit I assumed was decontaminated: a bright red dress, red shoes, beads, a large straw hat, sunglasses, bright red lipstick, a tiny white purse with a gold chain. It was a good disguise—I'd never worn bright red lipstick before, and the dress and shoes weren't exactly my style either.

The hardest part was not being able to hug my hostage-taker good-bye. Once the blindfold was on, I couldn't even see him. I didn't speak either, because I knew I'd break down if I did. He held my arm with a gloved hand and led me out of the room. All he said was "Twenty-two steps here" when we were climbing the stairs. We reached the garage and I climbed into a car. I wondered if he was going to be with me. I hoped he wasn't; it was safer if he stayed behind, and emotionally easier for me.

We drove for a long time. The tension I felt canceled any other emotions I might have had.

The car stopped and remained stationary for at least two hours, maybe more. I didn't know why and no one told me. I heard all sorts of noises—rumbling, voices, other cars.

Finally the car door opened and a gloved hand led me to the plane. I climbed on board, drank the juice they gave me. For a split second I thought, *This could be the end, it could all be a trick*—but I fell asleep before irrational paranoia got the better of me.

When I woke up I had no idea at first where I was.

Then I remembered. I was in the back seat of a parked

car. There was tinted glass between me and the driver, but the side windows were clear, at least from the inside.

What I saw through the car window stunned me. A sidewalk, buildings, people of all ages walking by. Signs, stores, noise. The world was vast; there was so much in it. It was completely overwhelming and I wasn't sure I was ready for it. *Oh brave new world*—where was that line from?

Ready or not, I had to follow the instructions I'd been given. The bench was just outside the door; I'd definitely need it. I was still in the twilight zone.

I adjusted my hat, pushed my sunglasses up my nose, and tested my legs to see if they were steady enough to make it out of the car.

Slowly and carefully I stepped out into the light. Even with my sunglasses the sun was blinding. I sat down on the bench and the car sped away. It was all over. I felt like someone suspended between two dreams.

The Holiday Inn was across the street. I was desperate to be in a hotel room, away from the confusing crowds. Even the traffic lights seemed alien and strange. In only three months I'd lost touch with everything I'd known.

I walked into the hotel, trying not to let my nervousness show, and made my way to room 2111. The key worked; I entered the room and locked the door behind me. It was an ordinary room with blue walls, a large bed, white curtains. There were jeans, a T-shirt, shoes, and a white plastic bag on the bed.

I looked out the window and burst into tears. I didn't

know whether they were tears of grief, relief, or tension—probably all three. I was relieved to be back in the world, relieved that I could see the city from my window. But I didn't want to be in that world without my hostage-taker.

I finally calmed down and undressed. While I was stuffing my clothes into the plastic bag, the phone rang. I jumped, terrified. I wasn't supposed to call anyone; no one was supposed to know I was here. Should I answer? What if it was important?

I picked up the phone.

"Room service," the voice said. "When would you like the meal you ordered?"

"I'll let you know," I mumbled. Talking to someone other than my hostage-taker felt artificial, as if I were reading a script in a play.

I washed my face and stared at the mirror. The expression in my eyes reminded me of my hostage-taker. Some of his seriousness had become a part of me; I hoped some of my hopefulness had become a part of him.

I stepped into the shower and tried to scrub away all possible clues from my body. When I was finished I wrapped myself in an oversized bathrobe and quickly set the bag outside the room.

Then I leaned back in bed and turned on the television.

It was like coming back to civilization after a hundred years. The ads, the shows, the news—it all seemed wildly unfamiliar.

I began channel surfing; I couldn't focus on anything.

Suddenly I saw Mom on CNN. It was only a photo, and I missed the news report that went along with it, but I was suddenly desperate to let her know that I was back, safe and sound. And yet at the same time I didn't feel ready to face a barrage of questions coming at me from every direction. They'd want to know everything, and I wanted to say nothing.

My hostage-taker had been right: it was good that I knew so little. It freed me; I didn't have to carry a burden of secrecy. Only my feelings of love were my own, and those weren't a burden—they were a secret treasure.

My heart ached for my hostage-taker. Somewhere on the planet he was removing all traces of me. I knew he was think-ing about me, but that only made it worse. I rushed to the door and opened it; the bag had vanished. The last tie between us was gone.

I took another quick shower, just to be sure, and dressed in the clothes they'd chosen for me. The jeans didn't fit all that well, but the shirt, bra, and shoes were the right size.

I couldn't stay in that hotel room another minute. I almost ran to the elevator.

I walked down the street in a state of stupefaction; it was as if I'd never been in a city before. I felt completely out of place, and I was surprised people weren't staring at me. I walked four blocks, as instructed, and hailed a taxi.

"The United States Embassy, please," I said.

The driver didn't give me a second glance. At the first red light I remembered with a start that I was supposed to lose the hat and sunglasses on the curb.

"My shirt's caught," I said, opening the door and quickly dropping the cap and sunglasses on the road.

The driver glanced at me through the mirror. I hoped he hadn't seen.

He stopped a block from the embassy, which was as close as he could get, and it was only when I paid that he squinted at me with a puzzled look on his face. I turned away, hurried up the street, and approached one of the Marines guarding the building.

"I'm Chloe Mills," I said.

And then there was a big hullabaloo.

I'm running out of time: soon I will have to submit my formal report.

And I will have to destroy what I've written on these pages.

But I had to write it all down; I had to relive it one last time before I face my life here. What I can't put into words is how desperately I miss my hostage-taker.

Today I asked Mom to show me some of the magazines that carried the story of my abduction. She'd brought a bagful with her to the hotel, but I hadn't wanted to see them until now.

We looked through the magazines together. There I was, on the front page of *All People*, wearing a white-and-silver dress. It was a flattering, full-length photo that Angie had taken at a school dance. Underneath the photo it said: *Who Are the Terrorists? / World's Hottest Bachelors Wait for Chloe / Her Mother's Secret Fear*. I felt as if I'd been transported into some sort of alternate universe.

Mom and I laughed at some of the stories. People who barely knew me pretended they did and gave interviews: a ski instructor who had given me one lesson, a neighbor whose dog I walked when I was ten. There were also ads for a scary Chloe doll, a book about me called *Chloe from Inside*, and *I love you Chloe* T-shirts.

Chad had been forced to retract his story. He was accused of fabricating everything, including the two dates we'd actually had. Mom's "secret fear" turned out to be concern about my diet. There were photos from my gymnastics days, including a few of me screwing up. "*She never gave up*, fellow gymnast

Liza Saturnov remembers." I had no idea who Liza Saturnov was.

The story *Who Are the Terrorists?* was based on speculations from all sorts of experts. A different set of experts analyzed the two letters I'd written; they were sure I'd inserted clues about where I was.

I couldn't read any of the articles all the way through. Apart from everything else, they were full of errors. Some magazines got almost everything wrong: a photo of me at age four with my granddad was captioned "*Chloe, at five, with her uncle in Seattle.*"

"It's my fault, darling," Mom said. "I said yes to almost everyone who asked for interviews. I was so happy they were interested—I didn't want them to forget about you. At first there was a media siege outside the house, but then the guys on top decided it was a security risk, and they sealed off the whole street with armed guards—can you imagine?" She laughed, but I noticed new lines around her eyes.

"Are the security people still there? On our street?"

"Oh yes. There are security people all around the house, and they've supplied me with bodyguards."

"I'm sorry, Mom," I said for the hundredth time, and for the hundredth time she answered, "I'm so happy to see you in one piece."

She said, "You've changed, honey. Grown older."

I want to tell her more about my conditions—what I ate, what I did, the movies I'd watched—but I'm not ready. I need time to sort everything out.

To the CIA
My report

I don't have anything to add to what I already told you about the ride to the warehouse and the ride back to Athens.

I don't have much to add to what I told you about my captivity either. The days were all the same. One time I got sick with a stomach virus or flu and my hostage-taker gave me pills and medicine until I was better. He told me his father had been a doctor and that he too had studied medicine a long time ago but his studies were interrupted. The chest I traveled in to the new location was an antique—I can try to draw it for you. I think there was a pool near the second location because I smelled chlorine. One night I thought I heard machine-gun fire, but it turned out to be a hallucination.

My hostage-taker told me he'd been in prison, where he was tortured. It was a dictatorship, he didn't say where, but he said the community was Christian.

It drizzled a bit now and then, and there were a few rainstorms. On my birthday he brought me purple irises and sherry. I often lectured him about taking the law into his own hands.

I don't have any more clues for you. My hostage-taker had a briefcase, but he kept it locked. He once took some books out of it— I think they were all in English, but I didn't see any titles. I already told you about the films I saw. I can't think of anything else.

Chloe Mills

Memorandum number: CM1172-13.
Classification: Secret
Subject: Preliminary Notes on Report Submitted by Chloe Mills
Prepared by: Dr. Geraldine Marlowe, Dr. Anil Rajan, and
Professor Erez Shaked

A. Chloe's Report

Chloe Mills took nearly a week to write her report; however, the resulting document could not have taken more than a few minutes to compose. Only a few brief details have been added to the information recorded at the initial debriefing.

B. General Comments

1. Brevity of report.

i. Most, if not all, released hostages remember and reveal many mundane details (e.g., food they ate, thoughts about their release, etc.), as well as the ups and downs of their emotional state. Memories of events experienced during captivity are typically very vivid and victims feel a strong need, even a compulsion, to communicate them in detail.

ii. Chloe appears to be exhibiting emotional detachment and depression, common symptoms of post-traumatic stress disorder (PTSD). General erratic behavior exhibited by Chloe also points to pervasive PTSD. Chloe has not contacted any of her friends or relatives, other than brief calls to Angie Shaw and her grand-parents. She has shown no interest in the gifts that were sent to her and has not tried on any of the clothes. She continues to wear the same outfit, which is washed every night and returned to her in the morning.

This erratic behavior suggests depression, guilt, and difficulty in adapting to her changed situation. Chloe has not reported nightmares, insomnia, or any other sleep disorder, but it is possible that she would not report these even if she were experiencing them. When the possibility of taking mild antidepressants or sedatives was discussed, she vehemently refused. It is almost certain that additional, delayed PTSD symptoms will appear at a future date.

iii. The brevity of the report may be accounted for by Chloe's efforts to protect her captors (see 4.i and 4.ii. below). It is possible that she rejected the idea of sedatives because she wishes to remain alert for that reason.

2. Compatibility of report with typical hostage scenarios.
The report is for the most part incompatible with parallel political hostage situations, and fits in more with sexual predatory kidnapping, where gifts and food may be given to the victim. However, it may also accord with systematic brainwashing strategies, used for example by cult leaders (see 4.i. below).

3. Compatibility of report with Chloe's physical condition.
i. The report is compatible with Chloe's general good health.

ii. No signs of torture or violence were detected. However, Chloe may have been subjected to forms of torture that do not leave any marks, such as confinement in a small, dark space, stripping, noise, dunking, threats, exposure to phobia-inducing stimuli such as spiders, etc.

iii. Substantial quantities of midazolam (one of the so-called rape drugs) and meperidine (Demerol) showed up in Chloe's blood, along with a smaller amount of diazepam (Valium), which may have been administered later. The latter seems to have been administered intravenously; Chloe either has no memory of this or is withholding the information. The drugs correspond to the report of sedation, which may have lasted as long as 24 hours, possibly even longer, if administered at intervals.

4. Possible explanations for Chloe's behavior.
As far as we can determine, there are three possible explanations for Chloe's erratic behavior.

i. Chloe has possibly been manipulated into developing a strong attachment to and identification with her captors. In this case, it is likely that she dealt with only one male captor, with possibly a charismatic personality. Using strategies familiar to cult leaders, such as food incentives, a show of caring and concern, ultimate control, inconsistent withholding / providing of needs, isolation (in this case conveniently built-in), physical affection, sexual seduction, infantilization, etc., Chloe's captors may have brain-washed her into experiencing feelings of love and devotion. Brainwashing and emotional manipulation are easy to achieve in kidnapping circumstances, especially if, as in this case, the terrorists are experienced.

ii. Identification with the aggressor is adaptive in hostage situations. Chloe may be suffering from the so-called Stockholm Syndrome and is therefore trying to protect her captors. Chloe would be inevitably traumatized by being helpless, isolated, terrified, blindfolded, and in danger of her life. The likelihood of deviant or disturbing behavior on the part of the terrorists is also high and sexual assault almost certainly occurred. Chloe would be inclined to give herself the role of willing participant in order to ease her mental anguish. In hostage scenarios, the syndrome typically fades quite quickly when the victim returns to a normal environment, sometimes within a day.

iii: It is possible that Chloe is living in a fantasy world that she created during her captivity and that the entire report is a fabrication. Chloe may have been kept blindfolded in the presence of her captors (this is the most likely scenario, for obvious reasons). She may have been confined in a small room or closet during her captivity. Certainly the tennis, daily outings, wine (!), computer games, and DVDs seem farfetched. Trapped, sexually assaulted, and deprived of sensory stimulation, Chloe may have passed the time by creating this elaborate fantasy. She would know that her report is a fantasy but would prefer to hold on to the invented scenario in order to delay facing the trauma of her ordeal.

C. Options to be considered

1. Continued questioning.
There is some urgency, as Chloe may have information that will be more valuable now than further on down the line. Chloe is tired and vulnerable, and it should not be very difficult to break down her defenses. A deprogramming expert should be on hand. Assessments based on Chloe's Pre-SAT scores and schoolwork indicate a high Intelligence Quotient, between 135 and 140. Appeals to her intelligence should prove effective, though she will also be better at contriving elaborate resistance strategies than the average person.

2. Delayed questioning.
This may prove to be more successful, as Chloe's feelings for her captors may fade, and her determination to protect them may weaken. If they do not contact her, she may be angry at them for deserting her. The predicted progress of PTSD will also make her increasingly vulnerable and open to reason. However, valuable time will be lost.

3. Enlisting Angie Shaw.
Chloe has by all accounts a close and trusting relationship with her classmate, Angie Shaw. It is recommended that a profile of Ms. Shaw be requisitioned, as Chloe may confide in her and Ms. Shaw might be persuaded to act as liaison between Chloe and authorities. Chloe will almost certainly experience an overwhelming need to describe her experience to someone so as to feel less isolated.

A more detailed assessment follows.

Washington, D.C.
Sunday, 3:45 a.m.

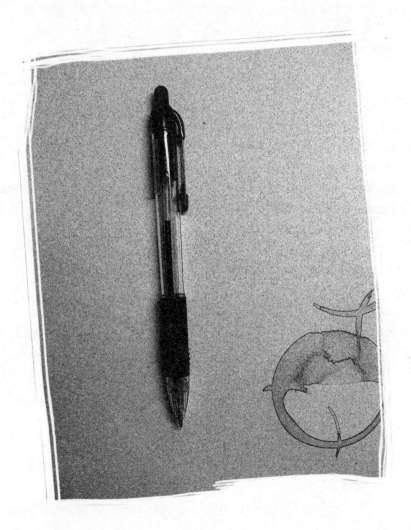

I can't sleep. Faint buzzing noises from the walkie-talkie of the guard on the terrace woke me. Or maybe my dream woke me. It was such a strange, vivid dream, almost like a hallucination.

I dreamed a CIA agent came into my room and began explaining that I'd been conned, tricked, manipulated—like the woman in *Gaslight*. He said everything that happened to me was a sting operation.

I shook my head and cried out, "You don't understand!" But he took me in his arms and stroked my hair and said, "We all make mistakes in vision."

I asked, "Are you his brother?" and he answered, "We used to be twins but that was a long time ago. But I love you too." I felt consoled and I laid my head on his shoulder.

He said, "Remember the sound you heard, of kids laughing and talking outside the warehouse? Why do you think those sounds ended so abruptly, instead of fading away?"

"You're wrong, you're wrong," I said. "It wasn't a tape."

"He doesn't want to save the prisoner, you know. He wants to kill him before he talks."

I was about to protest, but just then pieces of plaster began to fall from the walls and the ceiling, and I realized there was a war outside, and we were part of it. I looked out the window to see if Mom was there, but instead I saw dead bodies lying all over the street—men, women, children—piles and piles of bodies. And there were mourners standing around them, holding candles. The agent said, "They're mourning the end of the world."

I woke up shivering. Is the dream some kind of message

from my unconscious? Is it a warning? But who or what is it warning me against?

I know I have to get rid of what I've written. I have to soak these sheets of paper in water until they're in shreds. But it's hard. Everything is in these pages—my love for my hostage-taker, his love for me. I know our love will bring us together again. Love is the strongest thing there is.

Memorandum number: CM1172-15.
Classification: Secret
Status: Urgent

Memo to: Dr. Geraldine Marlowe, Dr. Anil Rajan, and Professor Erez Shaked

Attached is the document that was seized from Chloe Mills during the night. We had been aware that she was furtively writing what we assumed was a diary over the past six days. The papers were seized as she was about to destroy them. Chloe has been in a highly emotional state since the papers were taken and is under medical care.

Comprehensive preliminary analysis required ASAP, pending detailed report.